We, Jane

WE, JANE

AIMEE WALL

BOOK*HUG PRESS 2021

LIBRARY AND ARCHIVES CANADA CATALOGUING IN PUBLICATION

Title: We, Jane / Aimee Wall.
Names: Wall, Aimee, author.
Identifiers: Canadiana (print) 20210150092 |
Canadiana (ebook) 20210150122
    ISBN 9781771666701 (softcover)
    ISBN 9781771666718 (EPUB)
    ISBN 9781771666725 (PDF)
Classification: LCC PS8645.A46642 W4 2021 | DDC C813/.6—dc23

PRINTED IN CANADA

The production of this book was made possible through the generous
assistance of the Canada Council for the Arts and the Ontario Arts
Council. Book*hug Press also acknowledges the support of the
Government of Canada through the Canada Book Fund and the
Government of Ontario through the Ontario Book Publishing Tax Credit
and the Ontario Book Fund.

Book*hug Press acknowledges that the land on which we operate is
the traditional territory of many nations, including the Mississaugas
of the Credit, the Anishnabeg, the Chippewa, the Haudenosaunee and
the Wendat peoples. We recognize the enduring presence of many
diverse First Nations, Inuit and Métis peoples and are grateful for the
opportunity to meet and work on this territory.

JANE WAS DRIVING EAST.

Jane was driving east with a big, vague plan. They were drinking gas station coffee, eating pistachio nuts. They were talking grandiose.

We, Jane, they thought. We, Jane, they started a sentence. We, Jane, they spoke manifesto. They, Jane, were still aspiring to the name, one that slips and slides, one from which, the idea was, they would do the work.

But the thing was that, even then, even by the time they had made it onto the road, Marthe was still thinking of her companion as Jane and herself as just herself, always still scrabbling her way into that We, into that Jane, believing that to be distinct from the part of her that just wanted to crawl inside the other woman, into she, Jane. But Jane was not just her, Jane was to be them. Jane a great, shifting, multitudinous thing.

Jane's mantra: We, Jane, are only just getting started. We, Jane, are just a matter of time.

This is how they imagined it would go:

Is Jane there, can I speak to Jane?

And Jane's back. Jane's a baygirl who's been up in the big world and come home out of it, Jane's got less to lose than ever, Jane had wanted to be a cyborg, she'd wanted to be above the body, but here we are.

So. Is Jane there, can I speak to Jane?

Jane burning into the parking lot. Jane with a pickup truck and the knowledge and the tools. Jane's number scrawled on the walls of every virtual bathroom stall.

The first Jane had packed up shop. Jane's work, it was thought, was done. But really, Jane was always still just lying in wait. Coiled, ready. Like a fist you don't realize you've made.

Jane had told Marthe all her other ideas were no good. Too didactic. Marthe had been thinking herself an artist and this so much raw material. Jane told her she was never going to make anything good if she was trying to convince people of something. Marthe thought of all the ideas she'd been happily convinced of. How upfront were those agendas? She of course misremembered, she wasn't really sure.

But what if it's funny, Marthe asked. Then maybe, Jane said. But is that really your strong suit?

It was only when Marthe decided to write the Great Canadian Abortion Novel that she'd started having bad dreams. She had been imagining herself diligently researching, spending long days in the library surrounded by stacks of books. She had been imagining the novel as a great moment, a breakthrough, even as she wasn't entirely sure of the revolutionary nature of anything she'd have to say on the matter. She was focused on the saying part. But she got bogged down in the research phase.

Then she thought about comedy. She could do stand-up! This was the greatest untapped source of jokes she'd ever encountered. Why would nobody joke about it with her. They all shifted uncomfortably as they made laughing sounds. Marthe just wanted to joke about it. Take the piss out of the whole thing. She did, she really did, she had examined her own urges the way a woman who's been to a handful of therapy sessions would, just to make sure, but it really did all mostly strike her as absurd and strange. And funny! She probably couldn't get away with actual stand-up, but maybe it could be, like, performance art stand-up, Marthe thought. Funny in an awkward, painful way.

Google search: art projects about abortion

Google search: aborted pregnancy art

Google search: abortion art

Don't look at the image results.

A woman named Angie who live-Tweeted her abortion.

A woman named Emily who filmed hers.

A YouTube clip in which Tracey Emin sucks and gnaws on lychee berries and says about learning more about creativity from her first abortion than anything at art school.

A woman named Aliza who told Yale University that she had potentially deliberately miscarried in a serial fashion. The shit had hit the fan. How dare she bleed out of her own womb, her own pussy, what may or may not have been cells that could have become a baby. The piece was the story of the piece. Her senior project. *Are you sorry for what you did to Yale?* they asked.

And then, Jane.

She wasn't Jane yet but Marthe's backward gaze was Jane-tinted now. Jane, the sharpest eye in the room. Jane, a thatch of eyebrows meeting in the middle. She was itching and anxious till Jane.

Jane catching her eye. Jane really seeing. Jane inviting her along. Jane's long vowels sounding like home.

A sudden wave of vague, familiar longing. Knife-sharp and then duller, aching. This is how they'd do it then. This is how they'd do something, this is how they'd go home.

PART I

1.

WHEN JANE CAME INTO HER LIFE, MARTHE HAD been living in Montreal for three years. The move had initially been an impulse, an escape from an increasingly claustrophobic St. John's. She'd arrived with enough savings from her last restaurant job to float her for a few months, taken French classes, found waitressing jobs and people to drink in the parks with. Then she had decided to go to grad school. She never quite found her footing in that world, but she did meet a tall Danish boy in the library. Within three months, she had gotten pregnant, he had accompanied her to the Morgentaler Clinic, and they had fallen in love. Within six months, they'd moved in together, a Parc-Extension three-and-a-half they could barely fill with the suitcase each of belongings they'd both moved to the city with. Within another year and a half, Marthe had dropped out of her program and Karl had packed back up his single suitcase and moved home on a few days' notice. Her little Montreal life was stripped bare again.

Marthe was then working in a café that served lattes with

hearts drawn in the milk, and expensive eggs, the kind of place where people endlessly had their phones out, documenting their breakfast, taking selfies in the bathroom by the light of the bare bulbs hanging from the ceiling. The same couples ordered the same fourteen-dollar cocktails to start off every Sunday brunch; super-fashionable young women stole bits and pieces of the decor, walking off with a last cappuccino to go and the beautiful antique mirrors from the bathroom tucked into their supple leather totes.

She could get in the groove of it sometimes, weaving around the tables and the toddlers—so many strollers, suddenly, children everywhere—spending the morning wondering if person after person would like something to drink? *Un petit jus, un café?* Very occasionally she could even summon up something like charm and feel she was pulling off her part, the little Montréalaise waitress in the hip café, but her shifts were so early and mostly she felt old, exhausted by the idea of a cute outfit, a new cocktail.

She had asked for more shifts when she was dropping out of school, just months before Karl had left, and she'd gotten them, and the money wasn't great, but it would do. This was a period of transition, she reasoned, and she was trying to relax into it, to take this time. Swan around with lattes and flirt with the customers. But she was bored, and restless, and she was crooked at work instead and she knew it showed.

A trio of girls would often come in late in the day, clearly after jamming together in some nearby loft space, and Marthe would feel a sharp longing for their little gang, their bathroom-sink bleach jobs and matching stick-and-pokes and white bobby socks with beat-up black oxfords, their bikes and their ratty guitar cases and their carefully sourced nineties windbreakers. Their shared aesthetic. Marthe had lately been envying any women she saw who seemed to be part of a clan. The old Greek ladies in sagging knee-highs shuffling out of church together at the crack of dawn; the three generations of women next door in bright salwar kameez, sitting out on their scrap of grass in plastic lawn chairs, passing a baby around; the bright-eyed recent grads she ran into here and there who were always in the midst of starting some collective or other, to make films or performances or to start an organic farm. Marthe had friends in the city, but she didn't know how to convene a clan, so she told herself stories instead about how she was really more the lone-wolf type, anyway.

2.

One night in the early fall days after Karl's departure, after their break-up really, though he had somehow managed to skip the part where he actually had to break up with her by simply informing her that he had bought a one-way ticket home to his country and would not be returning, Marthe had gone to an outdoor film screening in Cabot Square. She'd gone alone, joining a crowd of mostly women sitting on blankets and little folding chairs at one end of the park, its usual occupants crowded out down into the other end.

The film was a documentary about a Dutch doctor who travelled by boat to countries where abortion was illegal, picking up women and administering the abortion pill to them on board, back out in international waters. They went to Ecuador and unfurled a banner off the Virgin of El Panecillo with a number to a hotline that would give instructions on inducing a miscarriage. It was all more spectacle than practical, really; it was media attention, the ship a galvanizing force for frenzied activists on both sides. But they were doing something. Marthe had heard about the ship before but hadn't known they were using the pill. She had been imagining a kind of miniature surgical theatre on board something that turned out to be the size of a crab boat. Really, the doctor was just there to monitor women who took a pill, illegal in their countries, that made them bleed. Adjust the blanket around their shoulders. All that fuss for that.

Partway through the film, Marthe noticed a man standing just to the side of the screen, facing the wrong way. He had dark circles under his eyes, an otherwise pasty white face, a shaved head. Camo pants and a scruffy black backpack. One hand on the handlebars of a beater bicycle. He was surveying the crowd. Marthe drew her knees tighter to her chest. The pigeons flustered around his feet and he was motionless, scowling. She tried to return her attention to the screen, where a mob of similarly twisted white male faces were spitting mad screaming at the little crab boat as it tried to dock in Poland. But the man remained at his station, just to the left of her peripheral vision. At a crescendo in the film, as the women on board tried to dock the boat, tried to find some way through the angry mass on shore, the man suddenly wrenched the backpack off his back and threw it to the ground and Marthe flinched, ducked her head. But nothing happened. He put one foot on the bag and kept scowling theatrically and the woman next to Marthe thrust her chin in the man's direction and then shook her head, and Marthe relaxed slightly, smiled at her. Shook her own head at herself. They were in Montreal. It was not likely.

When the film ended, a woman got up with a microphone to introduce someone connected with the boat doctor, and the crowd thinned quickly. Those remaining, Marthe among them, slid a little closer.

There was a dampening Q and A, a lot of fired-up audience members wondering how they could join up, as if it were a navy fleet, and the guest speaker smilingly shrugging that there was no real way to join up or work with this particular group, apart from giving them money and attention. It wasn't a fleet. Marthe wished they at least had ambitions of a fleet. Something. The crowd stirred and mumbled. It was starting to turn. Marthe was itching again. The women felt like she did, maybe. It had been two years, but Marthe was still angry at the indignity of it all, at the insistence of the physical body. She wanted there to be a fight about it. She wanted to join up but there was nothing to join.

3.

Marthe wanted there to be a fight about it but really, she'd gotten off relatively easy. Marthe had been pregnant for seven weeks but only knew about it for the final thirteen days. Thirteen days in which she had become obsessed with the now-glaring fact of her mammality—was that even a word—it was all she wanted to talk about, it had really only just occurred to her then, her mammality and her heavy little breasts and her bloated little belly, she had felt heavy, milky, full already. During those same days she had begun to receive messages online from a tall, lanky boy who had been, briefly, back home, a lover, years before, except she never would have used that word then, so European, he was a Christmas boyfriend, home in Newfoundland for a few weeks and then gone again.

The messages related the information that he had recently discovered that his dick could reach his mouth, or, Marthe extrapolated, that he had figured out how to suck his own dick, and did she wanna see? It was the first time she'd been on the receiving end of this particular kind of unsolicited communication and she had responded, light, giving benefit of the doubt: Dude, I think you've been hacked. But there were more messages, always late at night, that said no really though, what if I really can. And so she began to realize that this might just be a boy who had actually discovered how to contort his body so that his mouth could reach his own dick and he was so very proud of that feat that he thought she would be interested too, in the middle of the night in a city half a country away.

The thing she used to laugh about—she was careless, she drank too much, she'd always gotten off scot-free, and the thing she used to laugh about was that she must be fucking infertile or something because seriously. And then she was in fact very fertile, and she was convinced her belly was already swelling and her body felt so given over to this one purpose that for days after the nice Québécoise doctor pronounced her officially no longer pregnant, she was urgently hungry, like she had never felt hunger before, as if her body was going no, no, it was so full in here for a moment, fill me back up, fill me with sweet, soft things. She ate entire frozen pizzas, buttered white toast with milky tea.

The doctor had said tilted uterus, the doctor had said imagine the letter Q where most people have a P. Marthe had paused and the doctor said you have to picture *la majuscule*, a capital Q. Marthe liked the thought of the Q, but was mostly seized with a sudden flood of hilarious empathy for menstrual art, a new understanding, an urgent desire to smear the fact of her mammality, her aborted moment of mammality, all over the walls. She wondered if it might lead her to some kind of understanding of the urges of the boy with the contortionist dick pics, except for the part where he got to live in his body that way, so uncomplicated, so entitled, except for the part where that made her want to scream: Why does he get to and I don't, why does he get to and I don't, over and over, why do I have to, this life in this body, why does he get to and I don't.

She felt that someone had done this to her. The body. Stuck her with it. She felt, possibly belatedly, utterly betrayed by it. She read an autofictional novel by an Argentinian woman the same age as her who'd had an illegal abortion in a stranger's apartment. *A pregnant woman is a woman who cannot escape herself,* she read, and then she cried for herself and her own inescapable body, never mind the author and her actually harrowing ordeal.

The boy who had made Marthe pregnant was prone to existential despair. Later, she would sit patiently for hours as Karl ranted about feeling wrong in the world and how there was no point to anything, but at that stage they were still new, he was still restraining himself to the occasional dark comment, pissing hopelessness over some moment or idea that had given Marthe a sliver of light and not really understanding why she got so upset when, a week after the procedure, as she was still bleeding into fat diaper pads, he said as they walked home from some party that she was probably overthinking things.

Marthe had shut up about it but was left wanting to do something. It would bubble up in her regularly. But the way forward wasn't clear. People were less riled up and organized about something that had been legal for years, particularly in a city with multiple options for access. It was the precarity of it that got to her. How she was supposed to be grateful for the opportunity to make a decision for herself. How easily she could have been living somewhere where she wouldn't have gotten to decide, how easily it could still be taken away. But precarity was a slippery concept to fight. And Marthe had always been more of a joiner than a real activist, anyway. She was a body in the crowd, in the street, at the protest or the march. She shared the articles on the internet, she'd even written a withering comment or two; she went to the documentaries and nodded and murmured afterward.

With Karl's departure, the simmer of Marthe's restlessness had started roiling, fed by a new manic energy but still without real direction. So, she went to documentaries. She thought maybe an art project. She read about the GynePunk cyborg witches hacking reproductive technology in Spain; she wrote the first paragraph of three different essays. She sent unanswered messages to the administrators of defunct pro-choice groups. She went looking for a fleet.

And then, Jane.

4.

Marthe first encountered Jane at a meeting in a cheerful, many-windowed resource centre in Westmount. Brightly coloured posters brightly reminded them about consent and safe practices. Marthe had been imagining more of a church basement aesthetic. Folding chairs, instant coffee and Chips Ahoy! at the back, like an AA meeting in the movies. This room, in contrast, was relentlessly sunny. There was a beanbag chair. A selection of herbal tea.

The meeting was an information session for people who were interested in becoming doulas. Marthe was not exactly a person interested in becoming a doula, but she had heard that some of them worked on the other side, that there were abortion doulas now. Someone had posted an article about it in the Facebook event for the meeting, and Marthe thought oh, were they doing that here, maybe that could be what she would do.

She had walked into the room and immediately realized they were going to be made to do icebreakers and activities, and she felt the urge to flee. The group seemed to be primarily made up of well-off, hippie-ish white ladies in linen and long earrings, salt-and-pepper ponytails. When the round of introductions got to her, she stammered her name and said about the article someone had posted, and how she would be interested in exploring that kind of work. Four different women cocked their heads almost simultaneously the moment Marthe said the word abortion, and the facilitator said well, that is certainly something we can discuss later on if others are interested too. Marthe flushed and didn't open her mouth again. Most of the women had averted their eyes, they turned their attention now to the next speaker, but one woman across from Marthe in the circle of chairs kept staring at her as the introductions continued.

Heavy eyebrows, strong features, shearling coat, black jeans, black boots. Jane. Long, strong legs crossed ankle to knee like a man taking up space on the metro. Jane.

The woman didn't look away when Marthe caught her eye, so Marthe did. The woman could smell it on her, clearly, that she wanted to leave. This had been a mistake. Marthe didn't want to talk feelings, she didn't want to skip over the death and the blood. She was clenching the seat of her chair, waiting for a break in the proceedings, not bold enough to just stand and walk out.

They broke for tea and fruit finally, and the woman approached Marthe. She gestured at the tea bags and said want to come get a coffee? Okay, Marthe said. Under her breath: And not come back? The woman smiled, car keys already in gloved hands. She was older than Marthe had first thought, but it was hard to tell. Her eyes were thickly lined in black, her hair long and loose. There was something familiar about her face that Marthe hadn't initially been able to place, but then she heard the woman's long Southern Shore vowels and realized it was just that small gene pool thing where it was always immediately obvious which gate at the airport had the flight to St. John's. The woman introduced herself with a name Marthe would soon willfully forget, she would soon always have been Jane in every recollection.

Marthe followed her out to a dirty silver hatchback and they drove up out of Westmount and into Côte-des-Neiges, far enough that Marthe realized they would not be returning at the end of the fifteen-minute break. They got coffees at a chain place and sat on a bench in a little park near the mountain.

Not for you then either, Jane said.

No, Marthe said. I guess not.

They were sitting side by side, both watching a woman trying to coax her dog to take a piss at the other end of the park. It was too chilly really to be sitting still outdoors.

I didn't realize it would be so... Jane trailed off.

Me too, Marthe said. I was kind of looking for the walk you through the darkness bit, you know.

I noticed, Jane said, and sipped her coffee. Marthe sat up a little straighter.

I thought I was going to crawl out of my own skin, Jane said.

Marthe said yeah, me too, feeling emboldened, that maybe she had been the wrong thing in that room, but this woman obviously knew what was what, and they were on the same page, so.

I wanted it to work though, Marthe said. You know, I find I want to be in a group and then I always run away from it. But like, wouldn't it be freeing to give over to something, something bigger that you could work for, not just like, yourself and your fucking career or whatever.

She paused, wondering if she'd overdone it, she was too open sometimes, she ran her mouth. But then: Maybe that's why some people still do the church thing, Jane said. Something corny about looking for a church, I suppose, but there it is.

I'm from there too, Marthe said then, too quickly. From home.

Jane looked over.

I can hear it, Marthe said. Your accent.

And where's your accent then? Jane said, a mocking curl in her voice.

Oh, you know. It comes and goes. Like, code-switching or whatever.

Jane made a face.

I was kind of fierce about keeping mine, she said. But that was a different time. It wasn't politically incorrect yet to tell people they sounded like a fucking bayman and would never get a job talking like that.

She turned to Marthe. So, she said. What's the story then, how do you get up here to Canada?

Marthe felt like the ingenue in some old movie, stammering her backwoods origin story to the hard-boiled producer who's seen a hundred versions of her come and go.

And it was the same old story really, though in Newfoundland it had usually been told, mythologized, as the young man's coming of age. The drinking and the fucking and the thrashing around, looking for a fight or for something to keep you there, the struggle against inheritance and tradition and all the dead ends and the lost ways and the sappy songs and the stubborn pride, and then the realization, up on Signal Hill or down by the harbour on a foggy day or whatever, that it was time to go. Fade to black on a shot of a car heading for the mainland.

Marthe said as much to Jane, she was flippant, shrugging, and Jane nodded and said ah yes, okay, so you were going to be that person. And now what. A new mission. Or are we thinking about going home again?

Marthe shrugged. I don't know.

Jane with a knowing look, still nodding. I think we're the same breed, you and me. We could do something ourselves. Marthe had been smiling at Jane's grand tone but she still blushed an ingenue shade of pink at this.

Jane straightened abruptly then. Anyway, here. I'll drop you home.

Oh, Marthe said. Okay, well, if it's no trouble.

Jane bombed over to Parc-Ex in the little hatchback, driving so fast that Marthe was unable to resist bracing her hand against the dash. They pulled up in front of Marthe's triplex and Jane said here, give me your number, okay? Marthe wrote it on the back of an envelope Jane pulled out of her purse, awkwardly adding her name below it.

Jane paused, looking at the envelope when Marthe handed it back.

Whose affectation was that then?

She pointed to the "e" with her thumb.

Oh. My mother, I guess. But I like it, the "a" always looked so prosaic.

I was thinking you'd swapped it out yourself.

Oh no, Marthe laughed, as in she never would have changed her own name like that, and then realized there would have been a hint of approval had that been the case.

It was nice to meet you, Marthe said then, getting out of the car, inflecting it almost as a question.

We will talk soon, Jane said firmly.

Marthe went up the stairs to her apartment. She had kept the little place she'd shared with Karl, against the advice of her friends, who thought it was a sign of wallowing, that the place would be full of ghosts. But Marthe hadn't had the energy to move when everything first collapsed, and the place was cheap enough that she could afford it alone, and she liked it. She saw it as a way of standing her ground. She wouldn't lose her apartment on top of everything else. She'd just gutted the place of the remnants of Karl's things and had slowly started to spread out, take up all the space for herself.

She stood over the stove, picking at a pot of leftover pasta. She felt a bit like she did walking home in the early morning from a new lover's place, that desire to dawdle over a coffee and replay the events of the night again for herself. She finished eating and washed the dishes and then her phone buzzed, a call from an unsaved number. Already, Marthe thought.

So, I have an idea, Jane said as soon as Marthe picked up. I think we do our own thing, together, she said. Fuck that doula stuff, okay? We can do our own thing. I have a feeling I know what you were after there. And I know what I'm doing. It's a long story, but. It's called Jane. We'll be Jane, both of us. There's a story there, like I said. I'll tell you another time.

Marthe barely got in a yes, okay, before Jane ended the call just as abruptly. All right I have to go but we will talk again soon, okay? Marthe nodded into her kitchen as Jane hung up. Barely a minute later, a text: Good things. More soon.

Marthe promptly forgot the name Jane had when they met, recolouring all her memories, and they went from there.

5.

From there it happened quickly, easily. They talked all the time. Jane actually still talked on the telephone, and she called a lot. The first few times, Marthe was so taken aback she kept trying to rush to the point, the reason for the call. Oh, Jane was just calling, she'd realize, and would try to settle into it.

Marthe imagined Jane sitting at a kitchen table, or curled up in a wide armchair. No, maybe Jane would sprawl, those long legs on a long, faded velvet couch. There was an aesthetic pleasure in it, once Marthe had relaxed into remembering how to talk on the phone. She felt like they were in an Ann Beattie story from the eighties, or a John Cusack movie, a split-screen scene in which Jane would have the receiver of a land line telephone cupped between chin and shoulder. Maybe she'd twirl the cord with a finger. Maybe she smoked as they talked, an ashtray on the table, one leg stretched out onto another chair.

These conversations all had a similar format. Jane would say how she'd been thinking again about that meeting where they'd met. How bullshit it was, the whole tone of the thing. It was too careful, too tidy, too nice, right?

I mean, you and I know it's a different story, all of this, right, Jane would say, and Marthe would agree.

But it can be another way, Jane would say. It's already been another way, Jane would say. And Marthe would agree.

And just as Marthe was settling into the conversation, just as she was about to ask for actual details—what other way, exactly, did Jane mean—Jane would change the subject, or end the conversation. It was dizzying, but effective. Marthe was consumed. As much as she wanted to know more about what Jane had in mind for them, for this big Jane they would both inhabit, she also wanted to know about her Jane—she, Jane.

Tell me your life story, Marthe would say.

I don't think it works that way, Jane would say, dry.

Little-girl Jane, mouthy and shy. She didn't say much, so if she was forced to, you'd get a mouthful, suddenly, hurled. Then she'd blush with teary rage and rush off to hide it.

Marthe regretted every acquiescent smile.

Jane at twenty, tall and blowsy beautiful. Jane with long tangled hair, long strong legs.

Marthe thought me too now Jane, standing taller. Me too now Jane, maybe she'd grow her hair long. Jane got married in white cowboy boots. Jane got divorced in Jackie O sunglasses. Jane drove across the city in a shearling coat. Marthe always wanted more.

Jane had had a whole life already. Marthe still didn't know how old she was. She must have been in her fifties. Mid to late, at least. Her face. There had been a husband, there had been a band, a whole other life on the island. Jane had toured around singing Newfoundland folk songs when it was just really starting to be a thing again, part of the "cultural revival" she now shrugged at, pronouncing those words with loud scare quotes around them. It had gone well enough, for those few years, but she was only ever mentioned now as an afterthought to the more famous faces of that time, the Figgy Duff and CODCO crowd, if someone really wanted to fill out a list.

There was a picture in her apartment, tucked almost out of sight: Jane with baby-round cheeks, thick eyebrows knit, long hair lifted high in the wind behind her. She looks directly at the camera, almost taunting. She is wearing boots and a sleeveless printed dress and her arms are thick and strong. She stands sturdy in front of an old van, its back doors open. A thin boy is visible behind her, just off to the side; he is slightly out of focus and looking away. The young husband who eventually got tired of carrying her guitar. His hair downy, blond like a child's.

Jane was vague on the dates but told Marthe she'd moved up to the mainland sometime after all that came to an end. She spoke about it wryly and in brief, that time. It wasn't what you think, Jane said. Don't get all sepia-toned on me. But then, maybe it was, I don't know. She would say things like that but then tell a story about some show at the LSPU Hall that had devolved into a fistfight, a full-on racket, and how that was the summer they put the clocks ahead two hours so it was light light light till late every night and everyone went a bit squirrely, all this in a voice dripping with that sepia honey and Marthe would thrill to it quietly, getting to go to that place. The St. John's she'd missed, a realer real, she was convinced of it, even as she knew to be sheepish at her own nostalgia.

The photograph was tucked into a shelf of books in the hallway of Jane's apartment, a loose snapshot. There was another picture of the boy husband, standing on a rocky cliff, thin and slight but cocky, looking at the camera himself this time, a jut in his chin. Marthe had laughed before she could stop herself: he looks like such a boy! What she had meant was: he looks like he can't have been enough for you! But Jane had a soft smile behind her voice when she said well, he was such a boy. A sweet, raging, restless, eventually broken boy. Marthe felt a tiny bloom of jealousy at the intimacy of Jane's tone, the knowingness, even though the next thing she said was how they hadn't spoken in twenty years.

Jane had come up to the mainland and tried singing in other bands, tried to make a go of a different thing, but it never took, there had been a particular moment and that was that; she worked as a midwife here and there until they passed an act professionalizing it; she drank until she quit drinking and then she started it up again. There was never enough of this story for Marthe, she never wanted it to end.

6

Marthe went in early on Saturday mornings to open the café. This was her favourite part. The warm, lit café in the still-dark morning, polishing glasses and setting tables with the music on loud, the occasional conversation with the cook. She always resented the first customers to arrive, how they waited outside, peering through the locked glass door. Other servers showed up and talked about their Friday nights until they were all in the thick of the brunch rush and then they ran around mostly silently except to bitch under their breath behind the counter about this table or that. Marthe hated most of the customers, with their dietary restrictions and their photo shoots.

After work she walked home the long way, stopped into the bookstore and the thrift store, got groceries and beer. She got in the bathtub later that night, after abandoning any motivation to make plans or go out, and sipped a beer, and got restless again five minutes later. She leaned over the tub and reached for her phone and texted Jane. No answer. She texted Alexis, who did answer, who was home and pretty tired, who was maybe just going to stay in and chill but if she wanted to come over and hang out, she was welcome.

Marthe tried to reconfigure this invitation in her mind, make it sound better, make herself feel carefree, and then she got out of the bath and dried off, got dressed, and walked over to Alexis's place in Villeray. He greeted her at the door with a dutiful, impersonal kiss, he offered her a beer and they fucked on his leather couch and then he said she was welcome to crash there, if she wanted. He'd put his track pants back on, was queuing up an episode of some animated television show on his laptop. Marthe was unable to reconfigure that invitation, so she told him she had early plans and walked home. Jane had texted back: Coffee tomorrow, 11. We have things to discuss.

7.

Jane said there was someone she wanted Marthe to meet. Back in Newfoundland. She was at the café already when Marthe arrived the next morning.

The original Jane, so to speak, Jane said. I'll tell you the whole story. Jane was still on this, teasing the story, making Marthe wait for the right setting, the right moment. And Marthe was the perfect, eager audience.

It was the first warm spring day, and they were sitting at a table outside the café. Not Marthe's café, an older Italian one, where the baristas were all middle-aged men who wore gold chains, stirred steamed milk into tall latte glasses with hairy-knuckled hands. It was the first warm spring day, but they still had the terrasse mostly to themselves. Marthe couldn't help herself watching Jane eat a croissant. It wasn't that she was dainty, but there was an elegance in the assuredness of her movements, the way she took up space. It imbued everything. Marthe would admonish herself for watching Jane with a director's eye, but she couldn't help it. It was like nobody had ever worn a coat before, put on lipstick, lit a cigarette.

They finished their coffees and Marthe did not get the story of the original Jane. First Jane had run out of cigarettes and gone across to the dep for more. Then she'd checked her phone, answered a text, and complained elaborately about her landlord for a while. Jane rolling her eyes dramatically, leaving lipstick prints on her cup. Everything was urgent and important with Jane and Marthe felt her own restlessness quelled. She walked home from the café feeling purposeful, significant.

8.

Marthe could admit to this: Jane wasn't her first.

She had been in thrall to other girls, other women. She had mounted pedestals. She had succumbed to awe that made little sense from the outside, a fascination tinged with something darker. She had mounted pedestals, but they were not uncomplicated. She didn't want to be with those girls, she didn't want to become those women, not fully. She wanted to try them on, or absorb something of them. Their calm, their certainty, their audacity.

Once, in university, when Marthe was trying to write stories, she wrote a story about one of those girls and took it to a workshop and they nailed her to the cross for it. They had little sneering smiles in their voices when they asked just why they were supposed to be so fascinated by this banal girl, this girl playing at bad girl, bold girl. It wasn't a good story, but they were talking as if Marthe didn't know about the act. The act was part of it, knowing about it would colour in the dark edge of Marthe's fascination, but it wouldn't dissolve it. She had felt them all looking at her like she was some sad, meek mouse trailing along after the girl whose vulnerability showed itself by never showing itself, who swaggered around in impossible outfits and told you to stop taking everything so much to heart. As if those girls were different from the boys you kept loving even though they were so obviously full of shit. Marthe felt the class would have been prepared to buy that, or smile knowingly at it, the allure of his swagger, his fear wrapped up in anger, the show-offy petty vandalism or the bad hand-scrawled poems. They would have understood a story in which a boy with dirty hair and some crumpled Camus paperbacks and an affected manner of smoking a cigarette was painted as thrilling company, a freeing force. They would not accept that a similar power could be drawn from a girl who was just wearing too-bright lipstick or not smiling after everything you said.

Marthe had a feminist rebuttal to defend her infatuations, but Marthe also knew what she was like. She was not unaware of her tendencies. She knew she should shore up a boundary, reach for balance, but she also just didn't want to. Just let me dive in, she thought pre-emptively at imaginary raised eyebrows.

9.

Jane said there was someone she wanted Marthe to meet. She said how she'd been thinking about the space there, on the island, the potential.

Jane was coming for dinner. They had, up to this point, mainly spoken on the phone, met at cafés, where they'd have one coffee each and then go their separate ways. Jane wanted a lot of time, but it was segmented time, on her schedule. Marthe had invited her over for dinner and Jane had hesitated, then said okay. Marthe imagined them sitting long over a strewn table, opening a second bottle of wine. She wanted to feel indulgent. Hearty. She went to the market for artichokes. She braised a rabbit and pulled the meat off the tiny bones and tossed it with ribbons of eggy pasta, cream and white wine and the zest of an orange. She started cooking too early and when Jane arrived it was all ready, sitting there, and Marthe sat them down to dinner too fast. She had intended a drink first, she had intended this to be looser.

Jane appraised the meal silently, a touch bemused, poured them each big glasses of wine. They sat down to eat and Marthe was flushed with the sudden awareness that this was maybe too intimate too quickly, this eating alone together in her apartment, the air still heavy with cooking smells. The pasta was slightly gummy, overcooked. Jane did not comment one way or the other. She ate busily, heartily, she kept topping up their wine, she mopped her plate finally with a scrap of bread, and Marthe was happy enough with that.

After dinner they went out on the terrasse with the other bottle of wine and Jane leaned back in her chair. She said how living here, in a city where everyone has a little terrasse and it's warm enough for enough of the year that you can really use it, like a little outdoor room, that was what had initially made her understand what it was for people to move out to Vancouver Island, or California, to go west.

You look back at where you came from and think why live like that. The slush, the snow in May, the forever blanket of fog. There are people who eat dinner in their backyards all year long and there you are, barely able to go out in your shirtsleeves except for a few days a year. Those people become at home in their bodies, she said.

Marthe leaned back too.

I think of you as someone at home in yours, she said.

Yeah, but that was hard-won. I feel like you're either born with it or you fight like fuck to get it, but only after, say, thirty. Thirty-five.

Marthe thought about the videos she'd watched after Jane first told her about the band, which had been called, in its main incarnation, Hard Tack. There was next to nothing online about them. A couple of clips on YouTube. Jane singing at one of the early editions of the folk festival, when it was a janky little set-up in what looked like a school gym, a low makeshift stage with a big tapestry tacked up unevenly behind it.

Jane barely twenty, her hair in the same long, loose style she still wore, pinned up above one ear with a little black feather. She had a thin red scarf tied around her neck, the knot hanging low in front like a sailor's neckerchief. She stood at the mic with her hands in the pockets of a pair of high-waisted trousers, leaning back slightly in a kind of Art Garfunkel posture. The guys in the band were backing her up on guitar and piano and bodhran but the camera mostly stayed on Jane. Her voice was odd, it was low and complex but there was a way she was pushing the words out, a strange force. Marthe could see how she wouldn't have become a darling of any larger scene, next to the girls with lilting, effortless Celtic voices. There was something spiky about her even then.

Chelsea from the second floor looked up at them on the terrasse as she turned in off the sidewalk and Marthe waved. She called out, she was flushed from the wine and relaxed now that dinner was over and wanting still to be generous, big, one of those your friends are my friends people, she called out hey, want a glass of wine?

Sure, Chelsea shrugged. I'll be up in a few.

My neighbour, Marthe said. She hadn't told anyone about Jane. Marthe had friends who didn't necessarily intermingle, she maintained separate lines of relation, she lived in a neighbourhood slightly apart from where most of her social scene operated. She was trying to cultivate neighbours, but the voice she intended to be hearty and friendly often landed flat and too loud. The other neighbour in the building, a wiry older guy who had the rez-de-chaussée, had taken to sitting in his car in front of the apartment at all hours of the day and night. She occasionally saw him eat a meal off the hood, make a phone call in that particular Parc-Ex Greek-inflected Franglais, move a bag of tools from the sidewalk to the trunk and back again. But he was rarely farther than a few feet from the car. So that left Chelsea, who was glossy and remote and worked at a gallery downtown and often had crowds of people over, and if she caught a glimpse of Marthe she'd invite her down and then introduce her to nobody and leave her to fend for herself.

There was the sound of the door and Chelsea calling out as she came into the apartment.

Grab a glass on your way, Marthe shouted.

Chelsea stepped out onto the terrasse. She was wearing a smock-like black dress and clunky little shoes. She sized Jane up in an instant and then crouched against the wall, pouring herself a glass and lighting a cigarette in a series of fluid, practised motions.

How was your day? Marthe asked. Jane looked over quickly, her face closing up at the intrusion.

Oh, fine, Chelsea said.

This is Jane. Marthe, gesturing.

Marthe then volunteered the information that Chelsea was from Vancouver originally. Jane nodded, looked out at the street.

Chelsea, Marthe knew, had a big online following mostly, it seemed, for being very good at documenting all the things she didn't really do much better than anyone else. They were the same age but Marthe never felt quite fluent with Chelsea; she always felt that she was just barely passing. She was, despite herself, fascinated with Chelsea's implacable exterior. Her high-gloss shell. Marthe watched Jane watch the street, trying to read her reaction.

Chelsea looked up from her screen. Remember that guy from the vernissage last week? He's been blowing up my phone all day. Marthe gave her a sympathetic laugh.

Did your guy text? she asked then. Uh no, Marthe shook her head quickly. And then Chelsea drained the rest of her glass and said cool, I'm actually going to head downstairs, I'm beat, I need to crash. Thanks for the drink.

Bye, Marthe said, as Chelsea swept back into and then

out of the apartment. Jane said nothing until the door clicked shut and then said I was going to tell you about Jane, about where it all comes from.

There was a regal, petulant edge in her voice, like now she wanted Marthe to ask for it.

10.

Jane the First was called Trish before she was Jane.

Trish lived in a small cove on the island, hours from town, where Jane had grown up. Trish was where Jane went at twenty-five, already married, already divorced. She called Trish and Trish said why don't you come live with me for a while. A saltbox she'd done some work on herself. Dogs. She said why don't you come live with me for a while, take some time. I'll put you to work here.

Trish was a midwife, the odd woman. She was the only game in town, along that whole part of the shore, really. She taught Jane, she wanted to pass it on, she wanted to ensure a lineage. Midwifery had never really come back into vogue in rural Newfoundland, except in a few pockets where there was an established person and the young hippie types overlapped with people who hadn't gotten out of the habit. There had been some quiet years, but Trish owned her place outright, her mother's house, and she did this and that, a kind of informal home care for some of the older crowd, and she had her garden, and she got by. She managed to make her little life.

What I want to tell you though, Jane said to Marthe. We would perform the procedure.

Marthe stared, uncomprehending.

She taught me that too, Jane said.

Trish's mother had been the seventh daughter of a seventh daughter. You know, Jane said. She had the touch. A healer. Trish the sixth daughter, who should have been the seventh but for a sister who died at birth. But Trish stayed on when the others left home, she learned at least the manual skills. To be able to take over from her mother, to continue the work. So she was the midwife and she was the only place you could go.

I guess I just thought they were all so Catholic, Marthe said.

Honest to god though, how does anyone think it wasn't going on, really, Jane said.

So Trish did both, Jane said. At first, Jane had just slept. Shell-shocked still. She slept and she went out with the dogs and she used the side door to avoid any women dropping by with the glow on them. Trish was a good midwife. She was tall and strong and sexy in a soft butch way. The women would never have put it that way to themselves back then, of course, but they felt it. They were wary, socially, Trish was considered a strange bird, she was not invited to dinner or the baby shower, but they liked being close to her even if they didn't admit it. You could just see it, Jane said. Trish had these hands, an intuition.

The women who came for the procedure usually came to the side door too, and at odd hours. Trish would make it so they wouldn't have to run into any of her other clients, even though she privately said it wouldn't be such a bad thing to face up to, the bellies rounding where yours will not. She felt they could handle it, she wanted to give them credit. Those women would sometimes sleep over, if they could manage it. Jane had thought it was a lover she was hearing creeping to the bathroom at night.

In those first weeks, Trish would drink with her at night, once the day's work was done. She was a prodigious, hearty drinker, waking up fresh every morning; she could put it away, Jane said, and never miss a beat the next day.

Trish gave Jane a month, and then said okay, enough now, time to get up. Even then Trish was alert to the possibility that all her work would be for naught. It was the mid-eighties, Roe v. Wade had passed in the States, Morgentaler was opening clinics on the mainland and getting raided and arrested on a regular basis. In Newfoundland, you would have to jump through a series of impossible hoops to have a shot at getting in with the one doctor in St. John's on the one morning a week he'd deign to perform two or three abortions. But even if Morgentaler was ever going to make his way down, if Newfoundland was to get a clinic, it would still be in town and not everybody could get into town, and anyway, more structure and rules and regulation and official blessing was never what Trish had been after. She wanted a living matriarchal line of knowledge, to be handed down and down and down, over and over and over. To pass down the control but never hand it over. She wanted us to own it, Jane said. Trish was for the long game. There was always going to be someone with no ride into town, no money.

Trish never had much truck with the women's groups

and the activists. They were in town and up on the mainland; they were not recognizable. They wanted to articulate clear goals, work from within the system. They talked about incremental change.

But Trish wanted to burn it all down, Marthe said. I like this, she said, her voice quickening.

No, Jane said.

I did, Jane said. I would try to rile her up, get her going, but Trish just wanted a side road. She was focused on the there and then. The town. A practical woman. Pragmatic. Romantic too, though, her whole matriarchal tradition thing is totally romantic, of course. Jane's voice, indulgent.

Did she ever get caught, Marthe said.

No, there was no catching about it, Jane said. She was known. She was the odd woman, you know. That was still. Back then. She had the herb garden, she had all these salves and charms and tinctures her mother taught her. She was a bit different. Those bay midwives were always these sturdy no-bullshit ladies, there was no mystical moon goddess shit. And I suppose they knew she was gay even though nobody ever dared say it. They just gave her a wide berth.

Jane stayed for three years.

I feel a little bit in love with her, Marthe said. Or it's an allure. Were you?

Trish was never going to have a wife, Jane said. And she wasn't real into entertaining other people's curiosities.

Marthe heard footfalls shaking the spiral staircase outside, laughter and loud voices entering Chelsea's place on the second floor. The gentle thrum of a bass speaker.

Jane said what Trish believes and what I believe is important is that we have the knowledge in our hands. That we don't let it pass away from us. She said god only knows when the next man will get it into his head to start dismantling the system and the laws as they stand now, or okay, what about those pills, what if it becomes all about the pills and then one day, the pills can't get in? I mean, Jesus, they've got about a week on the island before the fresh food runs out the day the boats can't get in. You think that's not going to get worse? We need to have the skill. We need to have some control of it. Jane's voice was rounding richly now, Jane indulging in great oration, Marthe always suddenly remembering once again that Jane had lived in front of a mic for years.

What I'm talking about, Jane said, is heirs, apprentices. I'm talking about you having that in your hands now too. I fucked it up back then. I took off. I'll admit it. I can tell a tale on myself, I fucked off, but we can go back now. It's time. We can be Jane.

When Jane talked like this, Marthe felt she was being given a gift of a kind of permission, to make grand statements, to set out on a mission, to talk about inheritance and purpose and not feel sheepish. To shuck off the skeptical irony her outside life was steeped in and let her earnest believer self out. She would be Jane too. This is what she would do. She didn't press Jane on the vague details, the gaps in the story. She took the story as it was offered, she was eager, she did not cringe. Here was a place to join up.

11.

Sometimes Jane would drop Marthe back home and then call her an hour later. Marthe always picked up. She was consumed, she was going with it. On the phone then, in the evening, Jane would say again about the house. Sturdy, vulnerable.

She would say it was important that there was a kind of hearth to the whole thing, that they would work there.

Like a clinic, Marthe would say.

Like a clinic, Jane would say, but also not.

Right.

But seriously, Jane would say.

Seriously, Marthe would say.

So, we would be in the house. But we could also go to people.

Can we have a pickup truck, Marthe would say.

We will have a pickup truck, Jane would say. And a little boat.

A little boat!

A little boat.

It was a storytime in which Marthe was the child slightly too young to be knowingly tolerating a parent's favourite story but doing so anyway with that curious feeling of something else in the world making sense, another little piece clicking into place. Oh. Like that. Okay.

Marthe said her lines happily, asking questions as if she didn't know the answer.

And what would our days be like?

Our days, oh my girl, Jane would say, winding up.

We'd get up early, obscenely early. Walk the dogs, breakfast.

We have dogs?

We have dogs. Maybe even a whole team.

A dog team!

We walk the dogs and take a little breakfast. A light one.

We are very ascetic, Marthe would say, solemn.

Yes. Keeps the mind clear.

Then we begin, Jane would go on.

Maybe it's a day someone is coming to us. Maybe it's a day we are out on the road.

We do house calls, Marthe would say.

Oh yes. We cover the whole peninsula, Jane would say. And imagine in winter.

Snowsuits, Marthe would say.

Long johns. A Thermos of tea.

The truck is freezing.

If we can even drive it!

And if we can't drive it.

We take the dogs!

The dogs!

A team of dogs!

Does anyone actually have dog teams anymore? Is there even enough snow?

O ye of little faith.

Go on then.

Well, the thing is, it's not like we're the country doctor on a house call.

Doctor Quinn, medicine woman.

No. We're like the midwife coming by. The neighbour who takes a turn sitting at a bedside.

Or it's like one of those co-ops where you learn to fix your own bike.

Jane would sharpen when Marthe was the wrong kind of flippant.

Well.

But like a witchy godmother bike co-op.

Okay now.

Marthe would go back on script, the part she liked best.

And what would they call us?

They'd call us Jane.

12.

Marthe had finally heard the rest of the story.

Her Jane told it this way: There had been an American girl in town one summer. The early seventies, years before Jane had come home to Trish. A college girl, niece of a draft dodger and his wife, staying with them for the summer. Trish said you could take one look at her face and know she'd been sent away from something. She would go into the store for a can of pop and she was always at the cuffs of her shirt sleeves, fretting them down over her hands. A little black beret pulled down cockeyed over brown cowlicks, a slash of red lipstick. Serious little thing. She was always wandering down around the beach, smoking rollies, skipping rocks, dragging around a book, the boys thought she was stuck-up. The aunt was a nurse, or she'd been a nurse. She was a rare one who was easy with Trish, she was an outsider too, she'd be a come from away for the rest of her life, and they didn't have children, American draft dodgers with no children, the women were a little cool. The aunt took the girl over to Trish's the first week and said we've got a bit of a situation here and I was wondering if you could. A chat, maybe, or even.

The girl was voluble, suddenly, alone with Trish. She said she'd known for a few weeks, she said down in Chicago, at school, a girl had told her there was a number she could call, Jane somebody or other who could help. But before the girl—Jenny was her name—before Jenny could get her hands on the number, it was in all the papers. Jane wasn't one woman with a connection, Jane was a whole crowd of women and they did the thing themselves, they were busted with a full waiting room and a handful of them spent the night in jail. There went that. Jenny was crushed. She took the blade out of her professor's razor. Trish didn't ask why she was handy to the professor's shaving kit.

I was so disappointed, Jenny said to her. She said I also just loved the idea of this big multitudinous Jane. I like that idea too, Trish said. I can be a little Jane here for you now though, if you like.

Trish had learned from her mother, who'd learned from a doctor in a neighbouring town, a mainlander who was at his wits' end and wanted to wash his hands of it all, but with a clear conscience. He respected Trish's mother, and he didn't want to be cleaning up any more messes made with knitting needles or weird herb mixtures. He'd show her, and then he'd do the follow-up; she'd send the women for a checkup afterward and he'd play dumb. Trish had watched, assisted. All the other daughters had gone off to the mainland or up to Boston. They married and they had children and they didn't keep in touch. By the time Jenny showed up, Trish's mother had passed and she was holding the fort, Trish still only in her mid-twenties by then, but capable, ready. So Jenny was not the first, but after her, Trish was slightly less hesitant. It was always an occasional trickle, but they came. Her disinterest in groups and politics aside, she held on to the story of the multitudinous Jane, maybe just out of fondness for Jenny.

When I was living with her, Jane told Marthe, it was our little joke, our code: I'm going over to see Mrs. Crawley now and then I've got to be Jane after lunch.

Were you around for all this then, with Jenny?

No, Jane said.

Oh, so.

I was living in town. With my aunt. I went to high school in town after some shit went down, I won't get into all that. But I knew Trish when I was a kid. Her mother used to let me hang around their place, help in the garden or whatever, when I didn't want to go home.

But you know Jenny.

Yes.

We are not fond of Jenny?

That's neither here nor there. What we're talking about is the procedure.

13.

Marthe had made flippant, dark allusions to having some experience of her own with what Jane tended to call "the procedure," but Jane hadn't bitten yet. Marthe wanted her to ask, but she knew when she was being obvious. She finished her sandwich, Jane poured sugar into her espresso. They were sitting on the terrasse of the café where Marthe worked, a place that had lately been causing her anxiety. She was becoming more and more aware of the fact that she was living in a city where you could easily sit on this very terrasse for ten years, drinking allongés, watching the world pass. Rents were still cheap enough to allow you to mostly evade the hustle; you could sit around talking about projects you were never going to finish, keep getting the same haircut in ever-thinning hair. Jane had wanted to come and see the café. She felt it would be amusing, Marthe could tell that was the drive. She had come in unannounced and waved at Marthe behind the counter, and when Marthe finished her shift and joined her outside, Jane said I wanted to see you in your habitat here. Real little Montréalaise now, maybe she doesn't want to come back and be a baygirl. Marthe rolled her eyes at her, fuck off, but there was a little pleasure in being observed by Jane.

The story she wanted Jane to ask for was about how Marthe had been made pregnant by the most beautiful boy in the world. Karl loved D.H. Lawrence and Hank Williams and making little tableaux out of the odds and ends he found on sidewalks and in thrift stores, calling her to come see, come here. He was the first grown man she had ever heard say "kisses," plural, and get away with it. They took Greyhound buses to other towns and cities and walked for hours and ate the little sandwiches they'd packed, and he noticed everything and the world was so new. She thought he was the last man alive to really love the world in all its detail. Sometimes he loved it too much. Then he would lie immobile for days, chain-smoking and wiping his eyes with the sleeve of a ratty, baby-yellow women's robe. Then she was like some Biblical Martha from that story she hated, she clucked and ministered, she got up and went to work. Other days he called her name from the hall of their little apartment and then leapt naked from the closet, his hard cock bobbing, her delighted laughter spurring him on. She never got over the sight of his long, elegant body, she never got over the way her name sounded in his mouth. He told her she was lovely, and graceful, and he pronounced her name in this way that seemed to make a world in which she could be those things. One of the first times they slept together he'd named all the parts of her body for her in Danish, and she'd walked home damp and flushed, whispering the beautiful words to herself. Their speech patterns blurred with the city's and then with each other's, a particular private chez nous language. He took a speech from *A Midsummer Night's Dream* and turned it into a poem about her pussy. In Marthe's fantasies there would have been a day on which she'd get to hear him tell a little dark-eyed child about the sun and moon.

But they were new when she got pregnant. They were

at the very beginning. She said I need to talk to you, and he had a lick of fear in his eyes and she knew he thought she was going to end it. They were sitting on the bed in his cramped apartment, a Saturday afternoon, she'd insisted on coming over. But then he didn't flinch. He took it in slowly. He didn't ask if it was surely his. He just waited for what she would say next. He was waiting for her to deliver a decision and it was true she had already made it, she had one to deliver. But she wanted him to care more visibly, she wanted it to be not just her thing to deal with.

Then it was a freezing February morning and he was going to come with her. She was fasting, dazed. She walked over to pick him up and he forgot his ID and had to double back and she waited for him inside the front door of the unmarked building as the lone snowsuit-clad protester across the street shovelled out a neat rectangle in the snow for his pacing and sign-holding. She had put pajamas in her bag. A cheap black satiny top and bottom set. She had said could we maybe hang out afterward.

It had hurt. More than she expected. Nobody had said about that part. The doctor couldn't find anything on the ultrasound at first, but wasn't worried. It was a nice Québécoise doctor, it was all women in the whole clinic, and Marthe was grateful for that. The men in the waiting room with their heads bowed, not looking at each other. The nice doctor with her Q.

She hadn't cried until afterward, until she was lying on the little cot enclosed with blue curtains, a monitor on her finger that started beeping horribly every time she started to drift off, and she wanted him to come in, she could hear that other women had their people, there was a mother and daughter speaking Spanish in the next curtained enclosure, she wanted her person, could someone go get her person. And when he swept through the blue curtain and immediately down to her in the bed—she remembers the long arms in the grey winter parka, and she had felt detached until then, she had made jokes, she had been flippant, they had giggled in the waiting room—and now he swept in through the blue curtain and the arms reaching down to her in the little cot and then she cried.

He'd made her an omelette, afterward; she'd put on the pajamas and he made her an omelette and they watched movies in bed on his giant old laptop and she wanted to say she loved him. She wanted on this day after this inescapable experience to be in a situation where she already loved the person she suspected she was starting to love. But she didn't. What could she say. I want to love you. I think I might. She woke up in the night and he wasn't there and when she went out to pee, she found him in the tiny living room, he had three biscuits arranged on a little saucer and a joint in an ashtray and an espresso and a finger of whiskey all lined up before him and he was writing in a tiny notebook, she knew she was charmed by him. The roommate's dog tore apart the garbage in the night, driven wild by the bloody hospital pads. She crept out early and cleaned it up.

Marthe would have said to Jane how, a year or so later, she'd thought she should write it down, how she'd been afraid of forgetting the details. They were somehow important. How when they left the clinic the protester was still there, stamping his feet in the cold, his sign leaning on his shoulder, ENCEINTE ET INQUIÈTE?, and she'd joked about marching over and yelling NOT ANYMORE!, and then she saw blood red rage and the joke turned sour in her mouth, and later she would tell the story to others as if she had snapped back, it was better that way. The rest of the details she didn't usually elaborate.

There was another year and a half or so after the February day with the omelette and the dog wild at the garbage. That day, him rushing through the blue curtain, had become part of their mythology. She would say how that was the moment she knew about him. She was pleased by the story. Once in a while she had thoughts like, that baby would have been two by now, that baby would have had dark hair like theirs. If it had become a baby. It was a benign thought, though; it didn't have teeth, it didn't hurt her. They would have one someday, maybe. She hated herself a little for the precision she added. If it had been, if it had become a baby. She knew fucking well it would have been a baby. This thing where people think you can't handle the thought, that you made that choice. She was on the other side of making that choice and she knew fucking well it would have been a baby and she didn't want to pussyfoot around it. She had touched that dark place. This was being a human in the world, this was being a body.

Marthe had turned twenty-nine and then she'd turned thirty and she'd thought maybe in a couple of years. She imagined a dark, downy head. She imagined him singing to a baby. If it was a child after him, she knew they'd be in for it. The energy. He had been a wild child, he had thrown things across classrooms, it was that he couldn't hold it all in. He just felt so much. Lying around smoking in the yellow robe. He was overcome. Sometimes it was infuriating, Marthe going about her days and him overcome, but she loved him for it too. She said to her friends how having babies had seemed like this far-off abstract thing, how she'd been ambivalent, but now she'd been having dreams about a baby boy. She said how she looked at him and she thought to herself I'd do that with you. She trusted him, thinking there's a man who wouldn't take off, she didn't mind admitting that she didn't want to do it alone, and she thought there's a man who wouldn't take it lightly. But then he was a man who fled. One of his friends had used the word months later. *Il a fui,* of course he wouldn't ever come back here.

He'd left her. Months ago now, months before Jane. He'd said I don't know how to say this, but I want to go home. She had been learning his language, she had been wondering about his mother. He'd already bought a one-way ticket. Now when it dawned on her that she would very likely never see him again in her life, she had once again that feeling of oh, this is what it's like up here in the big world. People go back to their countries and your grandmothers didn't go to school together and there's no coming home for Christmas to that salty clusterfuck of everyone you'd ever laid eyes on jammed together in a bar smelling of wet wool, picking up where they'd left off. They just leave, and you never see them again. She wasn't home. She hadn't been invited to go home with him.

Marthe had, in the end, not made it hard for him. She helped weigh the suitcase. She cooked a last dinner and fucked it up and cried over the blackened pan. He got in a taxi on a bright chilly morning just days after he told her he was leaving. It was all breathless and sudden. He was radiant. Her tears sparkled.

He had gone, and Marthe had considered her own situation, turning from the window. She spent weeks in a daze, drinking bottles of shitty dep wine every night, falling asleep on the couch. Then she got up. She cleaned the apartment and she went to work and she went to the gym and she went to every single event. She was healthy and productive and manic and fine. People started saying to her about getting on the apps. Get out and meet some guys. Everyone does it, there's no shame in the story being that you met on your phone. Marthe's take was that the story was so much of the thing, though. Regardless of what happens in the end, it will have been a story and you at least want the story to be good.

Several of Marthe's straight coupled women friends got left in a similar fashion within the span of six months. The men reacting to their belated crises of purpose, which were all variations on a theme, by blowing up their lives and leaving the mess behind. It did not incite desire to embark anew on another coupling. What she imagined for herself now was less a new nest and more a row of women with linked arms. She was getting ready to really come back out into the world and she wanted an army to join. Marthe raw, open, ready. Marthe was ready for Jane before she knew she was coming.

Jane made her feel a new exuberance, like even her melancholy was benevolent and expansive. Marthe looked at Jane and wanted to tell her everything, lay it all out, from the very beginning.

Jane, I come from a long line of sentimental women.

Jane, I don't have an ironic cell in my body.

Jane, I don't know what to do with this deep well I inherited.

But was that the beginning, really?

Jane, I have to confess that it seems like I believe in fate.

Jane, can your body believe something your mind has talked itself out of?

It's not the romantic, hopeful kind of fate.

Jane, I want to live out all the stories, but it might be I just don't want to face my own.

Jane, I'm greedy for a thousand different lives as my own ticks away.

Marthe was wondering what would happen if she fully leaned into Jane's aesthetic, the matriarchal inheritance, the purpose, the duty. Marthe was wondering what would happen if she went right up to the very edge of the sentimental. Touched it to be sure of the distance.

14.

Marthe's friend Heather had run into her and Jane having coffee at Marthe's café. Heather's tone was only mostly joking when she said I haven't seen you in forever, where have you been? Marthe introduced Heather to Jane, who was already shrugging back into her leather jacket, who suddenly had to go. We will continue this later, Jane said to Marthe. And don't forget we have to discuss the plan. Heather had watched Jane go, then insisted Marthe meet up with her later on that night, the opening of some new outdoor market.

Marthe chafed at the idea, what if Jane wanted to meet, but she went. That evening she found Heather locking her bike near a green space that had previously been a nothing little park and was now dolled up and refurbished for such things as pop-up food vendors, bourbon lemonade in reusable cups, tables for sellers of jewelry and handmade soap, and the inevitable DJ booth.

Heather was from home too, up in Montreal studying at McGill, still new enough here to be thrilled with the feeling of living in a real city, with the idea of pop-up taco stands. She was a hardy, healthy-looking person who had grown up on the west coast of the island, she still looked like someone who skied. They hadn't known each other at home; it was one of those friendships based mainly on being in one place when you were both from another, a few mutual friends. They had drinks every so often, they went to see any bands that came up from Newfoundland on tour.

She hugged Marthe now, still wearing her bike helmet, a big tote bag on her shoulder. Bike shorts visible underneath her dress. She was flushed and grinning. I thought I was going to be late! I had to borrow JP's bike, mine got a flat, but I couldn't find the key to his.

JP was Heather's boyfriend, Jean-Philippe. She had somehow retained enough from French immersion in

Corner Brook in the nineties to immediately shack up with a guy from Saguenay upon arriving.

Marthe and Heather joined a ridiculous lineup that was snaking down onto the sidewalk. Everyone around them was about their age, by Marthe's estimate. They were all, at any rate, within ten years of each other, and the whole thing felt designed to be photographed and then dismantled. Everyone was wearing the same two backpacks, their ankles bare above the same pairs of sneakers. Heather was pulling her thick hair into a ponytail.

So, your friend seemed interesting, Heather said, inflecting it as a question.

Yeah, Marthe said.

How do you two know each other?

Oh, we just kind of met. She's from home too. She used to be a musician, back in the day. She's great.

Ah, that explains a lot.

What do you mean?

You know, her whole thing.

What whole thing?

Oh, I just mean, you know, she's kind of. Heather paused. A character. Dramatic, or performative or something. You know, her look, her whole thing. I mean, I'm sure she's great too.

Marthe looked around them.

This is starting to feel a bit ridiculous.

The line seems to be moving pretty fast, Heather said.

This stuff just makes me feel like a fucking sheep or something. Corralled by pulled pork and fucking cocktails.

All right, Holden Caulfield, Heather said, and Marthe laughed, all right fine, but still. I want to go to, like, a baby shower, or someone's dad's birthday party or something where there are old ladies eating white sheet cake. I'm sick of all these sexless graphic designers or whatever it is all these people do.

Oh, cause if we were coal miners and schoolteachers it would be a different story, Heather said. Sure you're just as bad.

I'm just restless, Marthe said. I'm not talking about people being "real" or whatever, I'm talking about, like, I don't know, obligation? I want to be obliged.

Heather said here, why don't you stay in this line and I'll go get the drinks and we can get through quicker that way. I'll meet you in the patch over by my bike.

Heather walked off all sturdy and calm, and Marthe raged inside. Of course Heather didn't get it. Heather was another of those serene, fresh-faced girls Marthe used to break her own heart trying to get inside of, to be. Jealous of their calm and trying to squeeze in and take some of it. Why didn't it emanate from them in a way she could catch? That containment, that quiet. That utter lack of a need for attention. Girls who never drank too much, never overshared, had really white teeth.

Marthe didn't care if Jane was a little bit full of shit. Everyone interesting was a little bit full of shit. And Jane knew she was anyway. Jane looked all tough and then she both was and wasn't. She had shaken her head at Marthe's apartment. Where are your lamps? The lighting here is terrible. She made an approving sound about an old army green jacket Marthe had inherited from a friend's long-ago boyfriend and so Marthe took to wearing it constantly. Jane said you and me are the same breed. Jane called other people civilians. Jane operated under the assumption that Marthe was an artist still percolating a first great work. Jane had gone out in the world and made herself some good stories, and now she was inviting Marthe along to create a new one.

15.

Marthe called Jane early. What if we went away from here, like sooner rather than later?

Two ladies had been killed crossing the road in the middle of the afternoon, Marthe was feeling the hot breath of traffic everywhere, she was feeling hemmed in. We can't live like this, she said. She was having dreams about delivery trucks bumping up against her bed, the driver some skinny asshole with a cocky grin and a phone glued to his hand. She was afraid to ride her bike suddenly, her body felt too soft.

Jane said you sound like you think everyone is out to get you.

Marthe said what if we went away though.

It was slightly hilarious, Marthe knew, to feel suffocated by this city, which couldn't sprawl too far, being on an island and in large part composed of three-storey brick buildings with spiral staircases and weedy back lanes.

But she wasn't going to tell about the city. Marthe squirmed at the accounts of most cities, by visitors and inhabitants both. The same portraits painted again and again, the same details fawned over, and how they always got it wrong because it's not just those elements, but it's not not them either. The frame was never big enough, it could never be big enough. And the gall it took to think you were the one who could sum it up in all its proper dimensions. A city, a person. The gall you'd have to have.

16.

Jane dodged concrete questions. She circled back again and again to the same vague ideas of making plans, of possibility. Marthe started wondering if Jane had any follow-through, why she was suddenly onto all this again now. Why now, why go back now. She'd been in Montreal for years. Marthe was not good at asking hard questions of people, but it finally came out, more forcefully than intended. She was agitated and sweaty after agreeing to a second coffee, they were sitting outside her café after a shift, and she said so why now anyway, after all this time?

What do you mean, Jane said, suddenly alert.

I don't know, just, why go back now? What's the impetus?

Well, maybe I was waiting for a sidekick.

Jane gave her a little sideways grin and Marthe smiled at this despite herself. Jane's tone was aggressively innocent.

Is that why you went to the doula meeting? To like, I don't know, find someone?

No, no. My god, girl. Not suspicious, I know.

I'm not suspicious, I just wondered.

I went to that meeting because I thought I might actually be into it. I can't be a midwife here and I need another source of cash. But then, well, you saw what it was like. But I met you anyway, and I could tell we were cut from the same cloth, so why not now. Get things going again. I'm not exactly up to much myself these days.

Marthe tried to repress the shining relief. Of course Jane's intentions were good. Of course someone had just finally discovered her energy and her potential. Jane really seeing.

Okay, Marthe said. I didn't mean anything by it. I was just wondering.

Look, Jane said, her tone softer. It's been a rough few years on my end, okay. And then you showed up, and I don't know. This is a good thing!

Okay, Marthe said, softening to meet Jane. Okay.

Jane's eyes were still searching, still seeking to prove. Look, she said again, now grasping Marthe's arm. Let's go for a walk.

Once out on the sidewalk, Jane said you know that I'm done with the whole relationship thing. I had enough of that for a lifetime. But you.

Me, what.

You could still do it, Jane said. The whole thing, you know. A man and a baby, etc.

I don't think I want that.

You did, though.

For a minute, but. It was context-specific.

And now you're in a new context.

Yeah. Now there are other possibilities.

I'm just saying, though, that, you know, if the previous context was to return, I'd understand if you want to take that road instead.

I highly doubt that will happen.

You don't know. I thought the impulse had passed about four times and you think I didn't suddenly start living out some desperate last hopes when the clock started ticking down. Probably for the best, but still.

Well sure, I don't know, but I'm in, okay?

Okay, Jane said. A man passed them on the sidewalk, the late thirties overgrown-child type, baggy shorts and hockey-player hair, sandals. He was just walking along, eating a donut, sipping from a big Tim Hortons cup. Marthe wondered what it felt like to live in the world like that guy did.

Let's get back on topic here, Marthe said.

Come over later if you want, Jane said.

17.

Jenny, Jane said later that night, had returned to New-foundland in the summers for a while. She had moved to New York after that first summer, she had trailed around after the radical feminists, she would come back up to Trish's with all these books and broadsheets and little self-published pamphlets. Shulamith Firestone. Anne Koedt. Florynce Kennedy. Kate Millet. Trish never read them. She wasn't having much truck with any of that, Jane said, but she liked Jenny, she indulged her. Jenny would come up vibrating with ideas and indignation, and Trish would light her cigarettes for her, smooth her hair, sit her down to a plate of dinner.

They became lovers, Marthe said.

I mean, Jane said.

She wanted Trish to come to New York. Trish could teach them all, they would start a movement.

Trish had said what if I just teach you and then you can go down and do it.

No, Jenny had said quickly. No, I'm not good with that stuff. And I want you to come.

And Trish was not going to New York. Trish was only in her late twenties at the time, Jane said, and she had never been off the island. Trish cared about the work and she cared about carrying something on and she cared about the town. She read the local news only. Trish was not going to New York. And there was Jenny all fire and fight, Jenny going on about Shulie and the meetings and the marches and she'd kind of arrived in time for the death knell of the radical movement, but that only incensed her further.

Why didn't you like her? I can tell you didn't like her.

Oh, I mean, Jane said. You know. What was she doing though really? She was a talker, mainly, never thought Trish would go in for a talker, but there you go.

They were sitting in Jane's kitchen. Marthe had bailed early on a party, texted Jane, caught the metro. They were sitting in Jane's kitchen, drinking bourbon, Jane blowing smoke out the open window. Marthe had been bailing too much, she knew it. Her friends sent texts about not having seen her in ages, let's catch up. Marthe knew she shouldn't cocoon like this. If she looked at social media she could shame herself into a brief burst of motivational energy to, like, get out there and be young and carefree in a city or whatever, but it dissipated quickly. Every party was the same party, every night out for drinks another night in which nobody talked to anyone they didn't come with. It was all so sexless and sterile, Marthe itched. There was no flirting, no nights that ran away with you; everyone she met was self-conscious, they asked each other out via applications on their phones, they stopped texting back when someone made the mistake of vulnerability. They did not indulge in joy. They did not get carried away. They were not even full of shit in any kind of fun way. It made her homesick. She kept meeting people who said things like I guess I'm just not that sexual a person, I mean, fine, but. The party that night had been goodbye drinks for a girl she knew from the café who was moving to Berlin and somehow knew a bunch of art people, who all talked to each other with little visible enthusiasm and a kind of cold laughter and ignored Marthe, who'd sat on the couch talking to the one other co-worker for forty-five minutes and then made an excuse and slipped out.

Jane said I think you're just going to the wrong parties. You need a new crowd. Or else you need to buck up a little. Tell some people to fuck off. Bring the fire into it yourself.

Marthe didn't want a new crowd. She just wanted Jane's kitchen table, Jane who was topping up their glasses, saying again about driving home, taking the ferry, she was saying about Trish, how it was time.

18

At the café, the lineup for brunch started before they opened. Marthe watched the crowd forming, two by two. She had taken to expressing her bad attitude in the passive-aggressive way that was the only outlet available, prolonging eye contact for just a few seconds too long, letting the complaints about the menu or the wait hang in the air before saying of course, my apologies, I will bring you a new plate, or would you like to try something else, or can I offer you a cocktail while you wait.

A man came in with his young daughter in the first wave of customers. She brought him a coffee, and a few minutes later the orange juice the barista had pressed for the little girl. Once she and the other server had bombarded the kitchen with the first wave of orders, blanketed the tables with lattes like they were soothing babies with hot milk, they stood behind the counter chatting with the baristas, complaining about the previous night's closers, gossiping about the regulars, and the man with his daughter stormed up to the counter. Where was his food, what on earth was taking so long? Marthe slipped into the kitchen and looked at the chits pinned along the line and came back and assured him that it was coming up very shortly. But how can it be taking so long just to cook some eggs? he insisted. There are so many of you here just standing around and it's still taking this long. He pointed at the two baristas. What are these people doing? He pointed at the other server: And her, what's she doing?

The man was starting to sweat. His expensive casual

button-down was looking damp. The little girl stood hiding behind his legs.

Marthe took a long breath. Those are the baristas, they make the coffee, she and I serve the tables. The cooks are in the kitchen preparing the food and they are doing their best.

Well, this is just not good enough, I don't have time for this, forget about it.

Okay, Marthe said. I will cancel your order then, and I'll just ring up the coffee and the juice and get you your bill.

The man looked at her, exasperated. What?

The coffee and the juice?

You know what, fine, never mind, I'll pay for the fucking coffee and the fucking juice.

Marthe printed the bill and slid it over the counter, she picked up the card he'd slammed down and pushed it into the machine and handed it to him, and as she did so she said also, there's really no need to talk to me like that.

Excuse me?

I said, there's really no need to talk to me like that.

Like what? he roared.

You're screaming in my face and there really is no need.

Marthe had never ever done this in ten years of waitressing, but she was trying to pretend she was used to standing up for herself. When he slammed the debit machine back down and left in a huff without another word, the little girl trailing behind him, her hands started shaking and her face flushed. The last of the surge of adrenaline moved through her, a momentary high, and then she felt drained. But she'd done it at least. She was going to be that person now.

Near the end of Marthe's shift, Heather came in and sat at the counter.

Hey missus, what's been going on?

Marthe was still feeling triumphant, if tired. She proudly recounted the interaction with the man and Heather said nice, and then what happened?

Oh, well, that was it. He left.

Oh. Okay. Well, good for you then!

Marthe winced at her encouraging tone. Anyway, she said. So, I think I'm going to go home for the summer. With Jane.

Heather nodded, was silent for a beat before she said wow, big plans.

People not from Newfoundland always nodded sagely when you talked about being homesick or going for a visit or thinking about moving home. Marthe knew they were thinking of the magical vaguely Irish place they saw on the commercials, about flapping clotheslines and fiddle music and the irresistible pull of the ocean or whatever. People from Newfoundland generally practically leapt across the table in their rush to tell her she was nuts, she was forgetting, she was starting to romanticize, what was she thinking? What was she going to do there? There were fuck-all jobs, and didn't she remember about everyone being up each other's holes and knowing everyone else's business, and how everyone was already after sleeping with everyone else, and how it would just be the same old shit. And the fucking weather besides.

But Heather was a nice west coast girl and she was polite in her concerned surprise. Marthe topped up her coffee and said she had to go restock the fridge.

Toward the end of her shift, Heather gone, Marthe got a text from Alexis, right on cue. He generally texted her on Saturday or Sunday afternoon only. She still felt a bit like she had ordered him up online, but maybe that was fine too. Alexis had come into the picture when she broke down and got on one of the apps, needing contact and rehearsing detachment. He had suggested lunch on a previous Sunday afternoon and then invited her in, offered her a beer, and confidently went in to kiss her. Marthe had never really known a guy like this up close before. He was really good at being a young single guy in a city. He rode a fixed-gear bike, he posted selfies with ironic little captions, he often referred to travels in Thailand, time spent in Berlin, he was a confident, skilled lover who was rough in the right places and soft in the right places and held her just right afterward and never really looked her in the eye. That first afternoon they had fucked for pleasantly surprising hours, in bright, sober daylight, and since then he never texted back right away but always eventually did, eventually invited her over at the last minute and she often went, got laid, didn't sleep over.

She was tired and irritated after work but she biked over to his place anyway. Alexis had a beautiful wrought-iron bed, feminine sheets with a soft purple pattern, a muted peach duvet. He was about her size, wrapped around her perfectly now, slipping into sleep. They had gone for late lunch at a place around the corner, and run into a table of people she knew from the café, and they had all chatted and Marthe tried to look at Alexis from their perspective. He was absolutely expected, his glasses and his tattoos and the good manners of a guy who has usually always gotten what he wanted. He was like Chelsea, he was good at moving through these worlds, too good, it was somehow embarrassing. Marthe didn't like feeling too of her generation.

Marthe had generally fallen in love with hot-tempered, attention-seeking musicians, or more aloof, artistic men who did things with their hands and often drove a truck, had a dog, or only used a flip phone. Those men found her a bit too much eventually, and she would mourn them without admitting that they'd actually had little to say to each other, or that they made her feel loud. She got into more trouble with the over-the-top talkative men, the show-offs, the cocky performers. Charm. Sometimes she thought it was no less sincere when someone acknowledged the artifice, the effort, behind their behaviour. It was truer. People put on shows for each other all the time. Marthe decided she liked it when people owned that. She felt tenderly about a man who showed off for her. The problem was that it didn't leave much room for her own little performance, her work, her own thing. Jane had some of these qualities and Jane was clearly kind of courting Marthe, in a way, grooming her for a role, but maybe that was different. At least it wasn't a man. Wasn't it different if it was about sisterhood or something? Jane wanted her to come along, to get tangled up, and Marthe wanted to be wanted in the thick of something. She wanted someone to be a little bit possessive of her.

Alexis stirred, and Marthe disentangled herself, got up, and got dressed. He walked her to the door and kissed her, distracted, and she biked home, made a pot of lentil soup, spooned it into Mason jars. She paced around, looked at the blank screen of her phone. She was irritated with Heather still, something about the afternoon with Alexis had left her itchy and unsatisfied, and she was tired of being on the verge of actually doing something. Marthe texted Jane and Jane immediately called her and Jane buoyed her up on the wave of plans again. Jane had been thinking and Jane felt Marthe was right, they should go sooner rather than later, and Marthe wanted to just fucking do something finally and she wanted to feel the wind of acting on an impulse, so she said all right I'm game, really. She said are we driving or flying or. She said about giving notice, but fuck it, they weren't getting two weeks. Marthe was feeling like time was short, like she was thirty and she had never really just taken off, actually done anything, she had spent her twenties waitressing and drinking too much and writing notes in notebooks for projects she didn't see through, and it wasn't enough. She had outgrown the methods previously used to quell her restlessness, the booze and the late nights and the series of some guys, but the restlessness was still there, resurgent. She wanted to go a little feral. She wanted to let it get weird. Jane felt like an acceptable gateway. She would let Jane push her over the threshold.

Marthe hung up and poured herself a drink and felt pleased with the image of herself in the headlong momentum of doing something. There was a wavery ribbon of apprehension about going home, but she told herself she was going home with Jane and how that would be different. We, Jane, they would say, clinking glasses, triumphant. We, Jane, are on our way home.

PART II

19.

JANE AND MARTHE GOT ON THE ROAD VERY early on a light grey day. There was a faint mist, a rare kind of Montreal morning, a kind that always made Marthe wistful. She had cleaned up her place and found a grad student subletter for two months; she had given notice at the café, awkwardly apologizing for leaving just as the busy summer season was kicking in, but firm, too. She had packed one bag, she was determined to lean into some kind of asceticism, she wanted to lean into Jane fully. There would be no photos posted online with cutesy captions about God's country, she was shucking it all off. Logging off. She was tired of the sound of her own voice and the sound of most everyone else's and she wanted to be cloistered for a while. She wanted to work, to surrender to a pure purpose.

Jane picked her up and they made one stop for coffee and gas and got on the highway. They spoke little. It was early, and Marthe was excited but also filled with a resolute feeling still that was something about duty, readiness. It wasn't the giddy freedom she usually felt getting on the road away from her daily life. Marthe indulged herself in the dramatic feeling of inheritance. She couldn't tell where Jane's mind was, if Jane was just tired or if she was busy resolving herself too. Marthe didn't know what all this looked like in Jane's imagination and for the moment she was content to be alone with her version of events.

Jane drove and Marthe daydreamed about the work and she imagined them sisters, or cousins. She imagined them in print housedresses, sneaking cigarettes on a back porch. She imagined them sighing together and then bucking up. Shaking things off till they landed as creases in their fore-heads and then smoothing night cream into those lines. The aesthetic was something about tempered expecta-tions. The aesthetic was something about the pleasure then being in the in-between, the outside, stolen moments. The aesthetic was having no choice about what must be confronted. The aesthetic was wild dreams of revolution incited in kitchens and back bedrooms. Hands unflinching in the guck of it all and a nail brush on the bathroom sink.

Do you have people we need to stop in and see?

What do you mean? Marthe looked over at Jane.

Your people, parents, family. Any stops we need to make?

I told you, my parents are up in Iqaluit for the year, working.

Did you?

Yes.

Right, teachers.

Teacher and nurse.

Right. Okay good. Now listen, Trish is going to need to know that you're all in, Jane said.

Well, I am all in. I'm here, aren't I?

Real commitment, though, Jane said. There's no playing around to this.

I am committed, Marthe said. I quit my job, didn't I? I'm seeing where this goes.

Seeing where it goes isn't what she's going to want to hear, Jane said.

Well, what does she want to hear?

I'm just saying, Jane said, her eyes on the road. How do we know you're not going to spend a few weeks down there and then want to fuck off with some guy or back up to the mainland so you can go back to drinking cocktails in a parking lot or whatever it is your crowd gets up to.

Marthe, wounded: My crowd?

I'm just saying, Jane said again. We're not going home to go back to town, we're going down the shore and missus next door is going to be up our arses and there's going to be nothing to be at half the time, and maybe you've forgotten.

You've been away longer than I have, Marthe said.

Jane didn't respond and they drove on in silence. Marthe flicked on the radio eventually, stared out the window, drifting in and out of a light, anxious sleep. The hours passed like that.

20.

And then it was dusk, a velvet green-gray darkness that seemed as if it were falling down in amongst the dark silhouettes of trees, blanketing the woods. Marthe felt hungry for it somehow, she wanted to ingest it, craving its softness, her belly raw from the coffee and the apples and the dubious nuts from the gas station. Eventually Jane said well I'd ask you to read to me, but I guess it's getting too dark now. Marthe murmured in response, she was straining her eyes on the road, she had tensed her body in surveillance unconsciously. The darkness was nestling heavier into the trees and Marthe was watching for big black streaks of moose, a thousand pounds of gentle herbivorous immediate death should they hit one on the highway. No moose yet, but once two light, fairy deer. Their eyes catching the headlights as they turned to look, unperturbed, Jane breathing heavy having jammed hard on the brakes. Marthe had gasped, and then giggled, and they stayed stopped on the highway a few moments longer, watching the deer lope off.

Now Jane looked over, spoke to the muscle in Marthe's jaw. We're still on the mainland, she said. There's not a ton of them around, she said.

I know, Marthe said.

But Jane was nervous herself, Marthe could tell, and she just shrugged, remembering all the nights she'd spent driving around in someone's car as a teenager, the whole night organized around tracking down a dime bag of weed with pooled money, smoking it by the river, and then driving in endless circles, everyone laughing and talking and Marthe periodically slipping into sensory overload, feeling the speed of the car, the way the high beams plowed a path for them, her eyes trained for moose, but also for the bright white of a cop car should one come into view and stop them and they'd all try to yes sir, no sir their way out of it, brazen naive.

They reached Halifax by ten that night. Jane said let's find a motel, and Marthe thawed a little at the thought, so *Thelma and Louise*. She wondered if Jane made those allusions too, how did Jane experience this experience? In Marthe's mind, Jane was free, Jane's experience purer, Jane just took it all in, took it as it came. Jane was not full of referents, she was present. Marthe found this thrilling but also suddenly irritating too now, suddenly it seemed like Jane just getting her own way, Jane always managing everything to go her way.

They stopped on the outskirts of the city at the first motel they saw. Jane said I kind of hate it here, let's just stay out here on the fringes. I don't want to go to some fucking fair trade vegetarian art school café.

Okay, Marthe said.

They got a double room and Marthe took their bags out of the car while Jane made a stop in the lounge, looking for a bottle.

Marthe dragged the bags into the room and sat on one of the beds, the reliably ugly comforter, relishing the moment alone, the blank room. Maybe she could just stay here, maybe this could be the cloistering she was after, the monastic. Let Jane go on and have a little retreat here alone. Write a Great Novel in the blank, dull room. Or lie in bed and sleep for a week. She stepped into the shower and turned on the water just as she heard Jane bang into the room muttering under her breath.

This province is so fucking Puritan, Jane called out over the shower. Even out here on the ugly fringe.

Marthe came out a few minutes later and was surprised to find Jane sipping from a coffee mug, a bottle of bourbon on the bedside table, a bag of chips open right down the front like a greasy silver platter.

I was persuasive, Jane said. And I overpaid.

Jane turned on the television and settled in on her bed. Marthe wanted to enjoy the motel, the chance to watch an actual television, the blank bed, the excuse to get drunk and eat trash. She stood at the window looking out at the street: three car rental places, storage facilities, a strip club, a Chinese restaurant. They had another drive and a long ferry ride before the island, but they were close enough now for Marthe's stomach to roil. The vowels would shift, the air would change.

I feel nervous, Marthe said finally. Like we've miscalculated. Things have changed there even in the time since I left, you know. And you've been away even longer.

Jane reacted so quickly Marthe flinched. She said really, now? Now is when you're going to come out with all this? We just spent the day driving to fucking Nova Scotia and now you decide that I don't know what I'm talking about and this is a stupid idea.

Marthe shrank, backed up against the wall. She said I don't know, I just wonder if we're a bit nuts to think we can just swan back in after years away and think we're going to bring the revolution or whatever.

You were convinced enough to come along this far.

Yeah, Marthe said. She wilted. I don't know. I'm tired.

Look, Jane said. Marthe could see the physical effort to soften her tone pass over her face. Think of it as us just visiting Trish. We're going to visit and then we'll see what happens.

That is literally the opposite of what you said in the car.

I'm giving you a thought exercise, Jane said.

Oh, great. Marthe paused. I don't even know this woman, she said then.

Well, I do, Jane said.

Jane was just as immediately calm again, implacable, unruffled. She said look, tomorrow morning we can sleep late, take our time, not much more to drive and the ferry leaves late. We'll sleep in and watch some crap TV and then we're going to go have a big breakfast, on me, and then we'll hit the road. Her voice hearty like she was already channelling the diner waitress. They were far enough east now that breakfast would be served by a woman who'd call them my love, my darling.

21.

At the gas station the next afternoon, the server said now my dears, what can I get for you. Marthe ordered bacon and eggs and hash browns that came in perfect previously frozen cubes, she drank three cups of coffee, she cleaned her plate, swiping the potatoes through a smear of ketchup, she was placated. Jane had toast and marmalade and waited to have a cigarette. Back in the car, on the highway, Jane settled another paper cup of coffee into the cup holder, pulled a rumpled copy of *Buddenbrooks*, fat with damp, from between the seats: Read to me?

Jane, Marthe had learned, liked big novels, Great Works. Mann and Stendhal and the Russians and Henry James. She liked novels of ideas with the ideas woven into the world of the book, novels where vaguely weak sick people sit around the sanatorium talking about time and philosophy and art. Jane wanted, always, the transcendent. The almost over the top. She liked opera. Most anything played by Glenn Gould. She was impatient with anything less.

Marthe had been thrilled to discover Jane actually read novels. Nobody read novels anymore, not really. And Jane's taste was somehow freeing. Jane didn't have much patience for the fragment, the autofictional, the contemporary confessional essay. She didn't have much patience for the novel interrupted by theory or some meta reflection. She wanted, unabashedly, her art to be beautiful; she wanted fire and transcendence. Marthe, on the other hand, had been raised on a steady stream of postmodern thought, surrounded by people who rolled their eyes at the canon, which was merited, mostly, but had also led to a certain amount of overcorrecting on Marthe's part that meant she'd been, naively, shocked to discover how much she loved Flaubert, or *War and Peace*.

Jane and Marthe had gone to the Musée des beaux-arts before leaving town. Jane had been reading about the Automatistes and wanted to go see them again before they left. They'd moved around the hushed room, which was empty on a weekday afternoon, looking at the big paintings that seemed at once totally deliberate and utterly free, and Jane had said how she couldn't get over how young they were, at the beginning, making some of these, signing the *Refus global*. They were babies. I feel so tenderly about them now when I think of it that way. Babies and their teacher who basically, like, heralded the Quiet Revolution. It was huge. And they were babies.

Though I suppose a lot of revolutionaries were pretty much babies too if we really think about it, she'd said, turning away from a giant Riopelle. Okay, she said, I'm sated. How about you? Let's get a coffee.

Marthe now took the book from Jane's hand and started reading. She loved reading aloud, it was so rare that anyone wanted it. She read and they drove on to North Sydney and Jane was quiet, listening. Her face was creased with fatigue now, she was nervous, she looked her age. Jane on the highway was not Jane bombing around Montreal putting on lipstick in the rearview mirror. This was not the wild road trip adventure Marthe had been envisioning, but maybe the whole thing was weird enough already.

22.

They arrived in North Sydney by early evening. Jane pulled into a Tim Hortons and told Marthe she could wait in the car. Marthe pulled out her phone and winced at the messages. She had mostly avoided looking at it since they left; if they were doing this, she wanted to really do it, she wanted to be free. She hadn't told anyone she was leaving town. It had been easy. There was so much to do, and people were busy. She'd given notice at the café, but just a few days' notice and then she was gone. Now there were messages from Heather, and Alexis. He was too cool to press, but Heather had sent a series that became alarmed in a vague, controlled way. Marthe sent off a few cheerful-sounding messages—got offered a lift home and went with it! might stay the summer!—and jammed the phone back into her bag.

Jane came back with tea and sandwiches for them; she drove over to a little gravel parking lot and pulled in. Crowded in there, let's just hang out and wait here. She settled the teas into the cup holders and pushed back her seat and turned to Marthe. So, you might as well tell me about the time you tried to go down this road before, she said. We've got nothing but time.

A night the week previously. Marthe and Jane walking through Parc-Extension and the cars flying past them on the little one-way streets and Marthe had stepped off the sidewalk and tried to cross the road, staring down some woman driving alone in a monstrous SUV. It had all welled up. I hate them, Marthe said. I hate every single one of these cars, I hate that we can't even walk around here, where we supposedly live. Look at them, they can't even slow down, where are they possibly going, why are they driving these enormous things with no passengers? She threw her arm out, just look at that thing. The woman in the SUV was tearing through the intersection now, nearly clipping a teenager with giant headphones on over her headscarf. You feel like a rodent, Jane had said. Exactly, Marthe had cried. This is not for living.

And the space! They just take up so much space.

You're not wrong, Jane said. My nerves are shot, Marthe said.

Do I sense a back-to-the-land phase coming on?

Give me some credit, Marthe had said. Then wavered, confessed: I've already gone down that road once or twice.

So, tell me about the time you went down that road, Jane said now, sipping her tea. You wanted a world from some guy is what I'm guessing.

Marthe wished she could claim that she had always had only a world of her own making in sight, but she'd faltered many times. Wanting some other. They were so complete and assured. The world she had wanted that time was about a teacher and a canoe and lace curtains in a little house in Labrador.

Marthe said I wanted to move to Labrador. Or, wanted, I don't know. There was a guy and I had this whole fantasy, it was all a bit on the nose. You know. Him tossing around the youngsters, cutting wood. Taking the canoe down the river. Picking berries, pulling potatoes. Like we were going to live in a Mary Pratt painting. He took me to Muskrat Falls and there was this yellow yellow light and I just thought.

What happened?

Marthe laughed. Oh, he came to town and dumped me right out in front of the LSPU Hall and the fucking Haunted Hike crowd showed up right in the middle of it, all those tourists standing there gawking at me bawling with snot all over my face.

Jesus Mary.

I know.

All right, look at the ferry schedule again for me just to be sure. Am I going to have to worry about you running off with some strapping young bayman then? The face on her, look.

23.

On the ferry, Jane led them to the seating in the front and Marthe watched as she started to set up camp. She was so contained, she created these little forts around herself everywhere she went and Marthe was always looking around. Jane kept her eyes forward and Marthe kept automatically reaching for her phone and then stopping herself.

Jane settled herself and then turned to Marthe. Sleep now, she said. We'll need it for the drive tomorrow. She slipped on an eye mask, tucked her coat up over her shoulders. Marthe pulled on a sweatshirt and sat fiddling with her phone, tired but not sleepy, and annoyed at being given orders. She waited until Jane fell asleep and then slipped out of the seating area and headed toward the bar at the back, still serving for another couple of hours. She got a beer and found a table and took out her phone for cover, and then sat eavesdropping on the low murmur of conversation around her, the familiar lilt and cadence of voices making low observations and other voices approving those observations with an inhaled assent.

Three youngish guys, around Marthe's age, sat down at the table next to her. Ball caps and work boots; they were almost definitely driving home from Alberta. They were in good spirits, loud and carrying on with each other, and when one of them looked over and caught Marthe obviously listening, grinning to herself, he said whadayat over there drinking alone, come join us sure, we don't bite. She hauled her chair over, hesitant and curious at first. Marthe was on her second drink and she was feeling romantic. How their voices were so familiar, these guys were familiar, she had grown up with these guys. They were quick and observant and they were always carrying on and they loved a good time and they looked out for you, she remembered climbing on the back of a skidoo or a quad and feeling safe. Marthe was indulging herself, how she still found the way the smell of gasoline and cold clung to your clothes after you'd been out on the skidoo vaguely erotic for its associations with the first boys she'd ever had crushes on. She was indulging herself but not unaware too that she was cherry-picking memories, that she was putting these guys at the next table inside the narrative with the boys who'd treated her like a sister to be protected instead of the narrative with the other boys like them, the other boys who'd worn their caps at that particular angle, who'd mocked her and mocked anything they didn't immediately recognize or understand, who'd called her stuck-up and a prude and a dyke and too big for her boots because she'd been shy in high school, read too many books, had the audacity to refuse the clumsy, aggressive advances of one of their own. That and the knowledge that she had clearly been sized up by these guys at the next table, recognized, deemed one of them, and that had she looked another way or been obviously from elsewhere it might have gone differently. But Marthe, feeling the warmth of a beer and a half, was on her way home and needed to tell herself it hadn't been a mistake and so she looked away from all that, back to the romantic version.

So Marthe hauled over her chair, she said Montreal, and they were all now b'ys, but then she said about home and she felt her vowels slide and they were all right on, they were clinking their beers to hers, they were saying how they couldn't wait to get home out of it. It was a relief to get this attention, but it was also jarring. These guys were familiar but part of her was holding her breath still, at first, part of her knew she was only going to reveal so much, that this would work, it would be easy with them, only if she kept part of herself tucked away.

Going home for a visit then, are ya, one of them said. Jason was his name. Jase. Jase and Steve and Lahey. They drank till the bar shut, they had her crying laughing, competing with each other to tell her stories, showing off, taking off this one or that one and taking the piss out of each other. She was giddy, she reached into her arsenal for every story she'd hung on to for when she wanted to put on her little baygirl thing in the big city; she had needed them to recognize her, she was thrilled when they recognized her, and then the bar shut and Jase insisted on walking her up to the seating area where Jane was. They had cabins and had tried to offer her one of the beds. I'll bunk down on the floor with skipper over here, sure, I'm not fussy, they said. You go on now and have a proper rest, and she'd laughed and insisted, no, no, she was fine, she was with a friend, she should go back to her. You're sure, they said. Cause it don't bother me one bit, I'm serious.

So Jase walked her up to the front of the ferry, it was dark up there, and quiet; there were a few people left up still wandering the halls, a father with a snuffling baby, a sulky teenage girl with headphones on, and he pulled her back gently before they entered the room, back into the dim corridor, and kissed her, a boyish, confident kiss, a good kiss, and he said maybe I'll just sit down here with you a few minutes more, hey. They sat in the back row and he put his jacket around her shoulders, it was familiar and strange, the smell of him, the little swagger of him, his arm around her then and Marthe was giggling, drowsy and drunk, and she leaned into his chest and they sat like that a good half an hour, his hand in her hair, and he felt it too when she started sinking into sleep, and he extricated himself gently, kissed her forehead, kissed the top of her head, and she watched as he swaggered back out of the room, smiling to herself. In the morning, Jane found her there in the back row, what did you get into now last night? And Marthe wouldn't tell her, she'd hold it to herself, laugh about it to herself.

24.

Marthe knew she was irritating Jane, that it was obvious she was hugging something to herself, and so she was extra solicitous as they got a cup of tea and waited to dock. Jane wanted to drive from Port aux Basques all the way over, one shot, and Marthe said well, let's just see. I mean we can take our time if we want to, right, no huge rush.

Marthe was half hoping they would encounter someone in need of a ride part of the way across, someone looking to go as far as central maybe, she wanted someone else present to shake them out of their own heads. A breather, a distraction. The previous night had also left her with an exaggerated hearty feeling, a more-the-merrier hangover. But nobody presented themselves. Jane had a look of steeling herself, now that they were on the island. They were really here, and it was really just the two of them.

What am I after doing with that red bag I had, Marthe said, as they got back into the chilly car and waited to disembark, and Jane pounced. Listen to this one now, got the boys to help you find your little Newf self again, hey? Didn't think I knew, did you? I woke up and you weren't there, so I went looking for you.

Oh fuck off, Marthe said, and Jane laughed. They drove off the ferry and got back on the highway and Jane said let's go see what they've done to the place, hey.

The cove where Trish lived was the latest place to be subject to revitalizing energy, another iteration of the hometown son or daughter returned from the mainland with money and ideas and designs on revival. In short order, such a town would have a music festival, a microbrewery, an artist residency, a restaurant where they told you the name of the guy who raised the sheep, a bunch of houses turned into vacation rentals for middle-aged tourists from the mainland. None of which were bad things, necessarily, but Marthe was skeptical when people suddenly started gushing. And maybe a little jealous, she could admit that much to herself at least.

What does Trish make of it all, Marthe said.

Trish is unaffected, Jane said.

Are you going in for the festival, the lady at the gas station in Deer Lake said.

25.

They drove across the island in nervous silence. Marthe felt anxious about running into anyone she knew, she stayed in the car every time Jane stopped for a coffee. They were on the highway and then they were on a narrow potholed road through nothing and then they were pulling into the gravel driveway of a little white house, a bit before the town proper, and Marthe saw lace curtains, tomato plants in beef buckets alongside the house. It was not beautiful, there was no real concession to the aesthetic, but it was active somehow, despite there being no one around. They got out of the car and paused a moment, and then a screen door opened on the side of the house and a woman came out, calling to them: She's just on her way home now. I was just here grabbing something, you can go on in and wait, I'm sure.

Marthe looked at Jane but there was no recognition in her face. The woman came over, she was short and brisk, she had blonde highlighted hair in a shoulder-length bob, she was in her sixties, likely, wearing a matching tracksuit, top and bottom. Don't mind me now, she said, I was just off for my walk, but I left my glasses. Go on in, don't be shy.

The woman bustled off, and Marthe looked at Jane.

Should we?

Let's run down to the store while we wait.

They got back in the car and drove down into town to the convenience store. Marthe waited in the car again, shy, while Jane ran in to buy cigarettes. Two kids with Orange Crush moustaches came out, an older sister in a T-shirt down to her knees dragging a smaller boy by the hand, bawling at him in a voice Marthe knew was borrowed from her mother: What did I tell ya, hey, what did I tell ya.

Jane came out after them and drove back past Trish's place and up a hill to a little lookout over the town. Marthe moved to get out but Jane just rolled down the window and lit a smoke.

So, who was that, Marthe said.

No idea, Jane said. She leaned back and looked straight ahead, still sighing, recovering from the drive. Marthe picked at a little threadbare spot on her jeans. Jane finished her cigarette and then backed out of the lookout spot and drove back down to Trish's place. This time there was a pickup in the driveway, and a person Marthe knew had to be Trish, a tall, broad-shouldered woman with short flyaway grey hair. She was already back in work gloves, a set of loppers in her hands, standing in a mess of alder branches on the side of the house. She looked up at them as they pulled in.

Trish didn't know why they had come, but she was not easily perturbed. Marthe could tell that much already. She didn't move from the car right away when Jane parked, flicked off her seat belt, threw open the door. Trish had come up to the end of the driveway and stood squinting, a glove dangling. Marthe's limbs felt thick and stupid in the front seat of the car; she sat watching the two tall women approach each other. Jane so confident in her reception, striding up to Trish, the car door still open. Marthe got out finally and followed.

Trish and Jane nodded at each other and did not embrace. Trish did put a hand on Jane's shoulder, sized her up as if she might have had a growth spurt. Jane said I brought someone. She said we came by earlier but you weren't home, there was a woman. Therese, Trish said. "Trease." Alliterative, Jane said.

So, who is she, Jane said.

Trish squinted. She lives over the road, she said.

Jane smiled, let it go.

This is Marthe. Jane, gesturing.

Trish, just glancing. She said go on in and have a cup of tea, I'll be in now the once.

Marthe had been imagining a warm, cluttered space, photographs and well-loved furniture, but Trish's house was spare and cool. It was a workaday house. The plants on a table in the kitchen were all things you could use or ingest, and they were primarily housed in beef buckets. The radio was on low. There were no photographs. Jane moved through it so assured. Beyond the kitchen, a little front room that was clearly never used, the sofa stiff. A daybed in the kitchen, the fabric of the long feather cushion worn smooth. Jane took off her boots and stretched out on it, Marthe hovering at her feet. Sit down, for god's sake, you're making me nervous, Jane said, so Marthe sat, and they waited.

26.

Trish asked no questions about their arrival. She had come in after them, set them up in rooms upstairs, put a pot of soup on the stove as if she were absentmindedly tidying. They had not fazed her. Trish a woman who will put on a pot of soup for a hundred prodigal daughters every time they traipse or stagger home, Marthe thought. Or maybe just one such daughter, just her Jane.

Jane at the kitchen table, in no rush to explain herself as Trish sliced onions. She leaned back in her chair, she was a bit proprietary, letting her gaze fall on different corners of the kitchen. Marthe was perched on the edge of her chair, alert, as if waiting to be called on. Trish at the counter in a plaid woods jacket and an ancient pair of men's jeans. Her face lined but still sharply defined, her hands strong and smooth. She was incredibly sexy, Marthe had heard it in Jane's voice but seeing it was something else. The energy. She looked to Jane, who was watching Trish too, she studied Jane's face.

Was Jane special to Trish or was Trish the kind of person who has a hundred special people? Does that make each of them less special? Marthe wondered about these things. She felt she was to let go of such notions anyway. Maybe she would be freer then. If we are all special then nobody is special then we are all special. Did it matter? Marthe wasn't sure. It could be just one of those holdover convictions she had never examined that would shrivel under the light of even the gentlest questioning.

Marthe stood up immediately when Trish eventually came to the table with bowls and utensils. It's fine, Trish said. Marthe sat again, accepted a bowl of soup, watched as Trish and Jane started eating without any further ceremony, and followed suit. Trish ate like every mouthful was owed her. Deliberate, like a task to accomplish, but not without pleasure, either. There was homemade bread. A sheen of margarine over the top of the loaf. Marthe had a feeling the bread came from Therese. Trish didn't say. A vinyl tablecloth with a faded pattern of chubby red apples, the kind you can wipe down with a damp cloth, sweeping crumbs of bread into your hand. They spoke little, ate busily.

Marthe got up to clear the dishes the second Jane and Trish had pushed theirs back. Trish waved a bored hand, just stack them over by the sink, she said. Marthe had waited until Trish and Jane had mopped their bowls clean with the bread before doing the same. They had all three wiped their bowls clean, it gave Marthe a good feeling. Put the kettle on, would you, Jane said.

There was an expectancy then, from Trish, finally, something like okay I've fed you, you've got a cup of tea, let's have it.

Marthe would have bailed right then, if she were alone in this, she would have backed away from every reason for coming, from all her excited chatter, she would rather have died than start pronouncing to this woman in her kitchen.

She looked to Jane, trying to transmit something pleading that Trish wouldn't be able to read, but Jane was brash confident, the true unabashed prodigal daughter.

Jane said I have brought Marthe so we can teach her.

Marthe shrank slightly, knowing she shouldn't. She should look tall, sturdy enough to bear a torch passed. She smiled instead, peeling her forearm off the damp vinyl.

Trish nodded.

Jane said we needed an heir, didn't we?

An heir-apprentice, Jane said again, smiling, after what seemed to Marthe like ten minutes of silence. She was astonished at Jane's light tone.

Trish nodded again.

The way things are going, she said finally.

The conversation was left there. Trish went up to bed early and Marthe relaxed slightly. She and Jane pulled the kitchen chairs out onto the scrubby land behind the house and drank bottles of Labatt Blue from Trish's fridge. Jane had helped herself. Marthe picked at the label. I think I was still expecting her to be kind of mystical or something, she said. Not her style, Jane said. No, I see that now, Marthe said. I don't know why I thought that.

Marthe trailed off, shrugged. She hadn't been alone in days and was dying to slip off and process all this on her own. She could feel herself wanting reassurance from Jane and knew she wouldn't bring herself to ask for it. Marthe had talked about coming home for so long and the minute she arrived she was mortified by her own words, the bullshit she talked to people at parties in

Montreal, effusive and flushed pink drunk, letting them believe she was at the mercy of the pull of the ocean or some shit, half believing it herself. Jane went up to bed and Marthe stayed out a while longer, shivering, staring up the road at nothing, before going in herself, up to the room Trish had shown her to earlier, a narrow bed, a comforter printed with small yellow flowers, a wardrobe, and a chair.

27.

In the morning, Marthe waited until she heard Jane's heavy tread in the kitchen before she went downstairs. Jane got up and took down another cup once she saw Marthe, gestured for her to sit, and just as Marthe was sipping the milky Tetley offered her, Trish poked her head in from outside, an old flip phone in her hand. Ruth, she said, and Marthe looked up, startled, as Jane responded. And something fell away.

Jane had so firmly become Jane in Marthe's mind that she was jolted, even though she knew, she had known, of course, all along, but you so rarely have to say someone's name really, and for Marthe, Jane being Jane was where the story began.

Marthe squinted at Trish backlit in the doorway. She thought about a night when she was eighteen and first away at university and totally taken with the one weirdo guy in her residence hall who was absurdly everything she had been wanting to find in moving away from home, an older guy in army surplus who played records for her and read her William Blake. She had gone with him to smoke a joint in a parking lot and then followed him to the twenty-four-hour Subway where, stoned under the glaring fluorescent lights, she had watched him order an impossibly bland sandwich and then eat each one of its components individually, feeling devastated that she would never be able to unhear how silly his giggle sounded now, that she could never cover back up the layers that had been stripped away.

Marthe had been expecting, after the previous night's dinner, that there would be a getting down to business type of meeting this morning. That they would lay out a timeline, make plans. How was this going to work. Jane, how were they going to bring Jane back. But when Trish poked her head in with her "Ruth," she went on to say that she and Therese had to drive down the shore and do a few things that morning, they'd be back later on. Marthe had nodded and sipped her tea. She watched out the window as Trish and Therese walked out to the truck, Trish a good head taller, got in, and drove away.

So what now, Marthe said.

I wonder how long that's been going on, Ruth said, because she was Ruth now, inevitably, it had been done, and all of the energy that had been driving Jane in Montreal, those long phone calls, all the insistent plans, it seemed to have evaporated. Ruth was going to drink her tea and have a smoke and she was in no rush to add much else to the agenda. Marthe felt a little sick but tried to look away from it.

Didn't I tell you there'd be some waiting involved, Ruth said, noticing Marthe still looking for an answer. I mean, this is the kind of thing, we can't just go out looking for it, you know?

She was flipping her pack of cigarettes over and over on the table, upending it on its side and then pushing it over.

Marthe could hear the tones introducing the hourly news update on CBC, the radio on top of the fridge turned low. She looked at Trish's plaid jackets, hung on hooks on a raw piece of wood tacked to the wall. She had expected a different kind of beauty from all this. The kitchen was chilly.

I mean there will be things to tell you, to show you in the meantime, Ruth said. But this is a long game. She got up and went to the door, lit a cigarette and held it outside. Marthe felt murderous suddenly, trapped, the realization of an impulse catching up to her. She would need to be occupied in the meantime, she had thought the project was clear in coming here, now what, Ruth was going to sit around relaxing until some girl showed up at the door. Like, you kind of had to fire the gun in the third act or whatever, didn't you?

Do people, do they even still know to come to Trish, she asked.

Are you going to sook now? What, because we didn't run into the front lines of something?

I'm not sooky, I'm just wondering.

I assume they do. Small town.

Well, maybe we should ask. Trish didn't really say, last night, whether.

If that information will be helpful to you, Ruth said. But it won't let us see the future either.

Why did you leave here the last time?

Which time, Ruth said, not turning. I've been back and forth here for years.

Oh, I thought. But didn't you say, I mean, that you'd left, the Jane time, when you were here and working and everything.

Oh, that. Ruth, sipping her tea, looking out at the road. I guess missus keeps her own place over there still, she said.

Marthe dug her fingernails into the palm of her other hand. Therese, she said.

Smart woman, I'd say, Ruth said. You don't try to make a husband out of Trish.

Marthe gave up. She drank her tea and she got up and she said she was going to take a walk. Ruth was staring out the window still, chewing her fingernails. Marthe went upstairs and got her jacket and came back down over the stairs at a run, she affected a breezier tone. Okay, I'll see you in a bit then.

Trish's place was at a little distance from the heart of the town. Just far enough removed that once you walked up to the little peak in the road, you could see the rest of the houses clustered together closer to the harbour. Marthe wanted to see the refurbished main street, see what had been done. She had heard about the town's makeover, the revival, about how beautiful, the restoration. The tourists came and gushed. It put her on edge, though she didn't have a coherent explanation for why, and she had resisted going out to the festivals, the new things, when she was still living in St. John's. Get in the house this minute and finish your breakfast, a woman's voice bawled out from a doorway across the street, and a kid about eight or nine crouched in the driveway of the place turned his head at the sound but took his sweet time moving. Marthe ducked her own head instinctively, walked on.

28.

The story in this town was of a young couple who had moved home from Toronto to open a restaurant as step one in a plan to make their hometown the next Trinity or Bonavista or Woody Point. They had not been shy about their ambitions, and they had nailed it with the restaurant, walking the fine line of making a place nice enough that townies would come and build a weekend around it and yet not too out of step with the place itself. Or at least, that was the sense Marthe had. They had gotten themselves a ton of good press and the story was just right, they were young and ambitious but not too big for their boots, they were on the news talking about being rural small business owners, about raising a family, about how they didn't want to turn the place into a baycation Disneyland, they wanted a living community. They were apple-cheeked and sincere and they had retained their accents or dug them back out after five years on the mainland, and they brought their friends and in short order one of them was elected mayor, and another had gotten enough grant money to open the theatre back up for a summer season. Buildings along the main drag were brightened up and restored, the place wrangled and finessed into the subject of feature travel articles in glossy U.S. publications.

And so townies in their thirties had started trickling back out to the cove alongside the new activity. Marthe was vaguely aware of this slow little wave via its earnest social media documentation. They were growing potatoes in their backyards and were very enthusiastic with the older locals and a lot of them were trailing toddlers around by the hand. Was that what Trish had been talking about? That where there are toddlers there will be women not wanting another, or any at all. On paper, Marthe was mostly for all of this, but she felt a kind of embarrassment about her eager peers, their essentially romantic ideas. She felt an urge to differentiate herself from them, but she also knew she was full of shit if she even tried. Or tried to deny that she had wanted some of it herself, on some level. The Labrador story she had only given Jane the broad strokes of. At least she knew she was full of shit. Marthe had a sense of shame if nothing else.

The colours brightened as Marthe reached the main drag. The restoration of these buildings had gotten the hoped-for attention. If they could do it out in Bonavista and get the people to come, then why not here: that had been the party line. Sure, it was just as beautiful here. These buildings now housed a gallery and a little museum and a theatre, a café and the inevitable crafts and knick-knack shops. Descriptions of the restoration work had always made Marthe think of those Western film sets with the empty facades, but she had to admit as she approached that the buildings were beautiful, if somehow a little too-too. Every heritage restoration project in Newfoundland gave her that same feeling, that the people hadn't realized that half the charm and interest was in the actually old, the faded and peeling, the unpolished. Everything was always fresh tole-paint colours and new laminate flooring. There was nobody else out on the road, and Marthe felt conspicuous, hating the idea of being taken for a tourist, regretting the second-hand bomber jacket she'd brought with her. She could go into the café, but they might want to chat. What would she tell people? She hadn't talked about this with Jane. Ruth. They had talked all this talk and made all these plans and the actual people in the actual town had been a bit beside the point.

Marthe decided she was being ridiculous. She went into the café and ordered a coffee from the bored teenage girl behind the counter and sat at a table in the front window, pulling the thin regional newspaper over. The girl behind the counter went back to her phone. Marthe tried to imagine her coming to Trish, "in trouble" and looking for help. It was a difficult exercise.

She drank her coffee and watched out the window, curious about the way the town worked now despite herself. But nobody walked by. A few cars passed, a well-dressed older tourist couple came in looking for information about a boat tour and the teenage girl turned solicitous and helpful, these were bread and butter customers, and finally Marthe got up to start the walk back to Trish's and to Ruth, with whom she no longer knew how to be without all the proclamations and the exhortations, their We,

Jane declarations, facing what she had sidelong known the whole time, which was that Ruth had supplied the Jane fire and Marthe had simply peopled the We.

Just past the café was the famous restaurant. Marthe hadn't noticed it on the way down, but she recognized the name now, noted the clean, contemporary graphic design of the sign, the font alone a dead giveaway that it was a business owned by someone under thirty-five. She saw a man and a woman around her age unloading stock from a little white van beside the building. A young cook in kitchen blacks was squat down on a milk crate, smoking. Marthe panicked and put her head down and sped past on the other side of the road, feeling foolish but not ready to face her contemporaries. The girl had a kerchief tied around her hair, she had a ruddy complexion, a loud voice. The guy was in a plaid coat and work pants. They wore identical Blundstone boots. Marthe bet they had a dog at home too. A dog and a homebrew set-up and probably they would soon have a baby that they'd put in little knit fisherman's caps and I'se the B'y onesies.

They didn't notice Marthe but she still picked up her pace, ducking into her coat collar, feeling ridiculous and faintly guilty. She turned off and wandered down to the beach instead of going home, she walked and walked and then sat on a log by the remnants of someone's beach fire till she was shivering, she tried to consider her situation, she tried to adjust the story.

29.

A truck slowed beside Marthe as she was headed back over the road to Trish's. Therese. No Trish. Here, hop in, Therese said.

Marthe hesitated but then obeyed. Trish is gone over to see Mrs. O'Leary and Ruth went with her, they took Ruth's car, Therese said. Yes, we were halfway down the shore and Trish got a call, missus took a bad turn this morning, fine now, she's after regaining herself, but she got a fright so we turned around and Trish went up to see her. That's Ruth's aunt, right. By marriage, that is, course Kev's been gone now three years.

Therese rattled all this off to Marthe as if Marthe were a person who knew about Ruth's family tree. Oh, right, Marthe said. She felt absurdly self-conscious sitting in the truck pretending she knew from Mrs. O'Leary, even though Therese, of any of them, was familiar. Therese was recognizable, Therese was much like most of the women Marthe had grown up around.

Therese pulled the truck in at her own place and looked over at Marthe. You come in and have a bit of supper with me. I'd say they'll be down there a while yet.

Therese's house was full of carpet and textures and cushions and doilies where Trish's was spare. Therese had the bay lady house Marthe expected. The photographs, gold-framed, of children and grandchildren. A crucifix above the door. A lace tablecloth covered in a plastic sheath on the kitchen table. Therese was efficient, she had cold ham, potato salad. You're not a vegetarian are you? she said suddenly, worried. No, no, Marthe said. That looks lovely.

My daughter-in-law is a vegetarian, see, Therese said as she sat down. And I'm after forgetting that many times to take out a bit of dinner separate for her.

Do they live around here? Marthe asked.

No, they're gone up on the mainland now a couple years. Come home every summer, though.

Marthe nodded, cut a tidy square of ham.

Therese looked over at her. I was married, she said. Years ago. He went up to Alberta, never came home out of it. The boys were still young.

Marthe nodded again, flustered at the thought Therese was assuming she was about to ask.

Yes, and then my oldest married a girl from here and they were going to try to make a go of it here for a while. I moved up so I'd be around to help with the kids and that. But it's not an easy go.

Therese sipped her tea and laughed at Marthe's face. You're not being nosy if I volunteer the information, my darling. Sure I got nothing to hide.

Marthe laughed, sat back in her chair a little.

Therese settled in now too. Trish came for the birth of my grandson, she said. We got into a bit of a pinch, he come early and we were caught off guard. The plan was to go to the hospital up the shore but it all went haywire. Anyway, someone knew to call her and turns out I wasn't a bad hand at helping.

Therese pointed to a photo Marthe hadn't noticed, stuck to the fridge. Therese and Trish on a snowmobile, red-cheeked, squinting at the camera.

I tried to get her to come to cards, and then I tried to get her to come to supper, and finally I got her out on the snow machine, Therese said with a low, pleased laugh. She wasn't too sure about it, but she came along finally. We went and had a mug-up in the woods and we've kept on together since.

Marthe laughed too, looking at the photo. Trish, in snow pants with the suspenders pulled up over a sweater, sitting on the back of the snowmobile, holding on to Therese, looking slightly concerned. This was a new angle.

And so, do you, um, like is it busy these days with all that? Lots of people wanting a midwife?

No, no, I wouldn't say busy. Here and there. Bit of a younger crowd around here these days though, so we'll see.

Therese put another slice of ham on Marthe's plate.

And, so.

You're wondering about the abortions?

Marthe had expected more euphemism. There was a crucifix over the door. But Therese said abortion in the same tone Marthe had heard her use earlier talking about Mrs. O'Leary and her dialysis.

Yeah.

Well, again, rare, but you know.

Marthe imagined Therese fussing over some young woman whose mother she went to church with.

That stuff we don't go round saying to everyone of course, Therese said then.

Yes, right, of course. Ah, Ruth told me. She thought, they said, about maybe teaching me.

Therese smiled. Yes, Trish told me how the two of them

are always going on about passing it on. This is the first I've met Ruth, though I've heard tell of all her many plans, and then there's the other one when she comes up, though she takes a bit of a different tack.

The other one?

Jenny, Therese said. Down in New York.

Oh, she comes up?

Oh yes, Therese said. Authoritative. Yes, sure, she's been up now I think every summer for years. Or at least so long as I've been out here, and according to Trish before that too.

But there's not a lot of, ah, business.

Well, no, I mean it's not people's first instinct anymore to go looking on the sly. Bit of a just in case situation here now. Could be hard to keep a trip into St. John's a secret, depending on your situation, right. So it doesn't hurt to have someone around. And god only knows what we're in for in the future.

Marthe paused for too long, taking this in.

You're looking dismayed, don't worry. I do think it's a good idea, them teaching you. I never wanted to take on the real learning of it myself, then you're on the hook. Then you have to come when you're called on and I had enough people after me for this or that in my life now already.

Therese cleared their plates and put the kettle back on and made two more cups of tea. She said let's go in and watch the news now. Marthe followed her into the front room, this one plush and lived-in, and curled into the other corner of the couch. Therese put on a pair of reading glasses and took out an adult colouring book and a little pencil case. Bit silly, I know, she said, looking over at Marthe. My son sent me up a few of these and I finds it relaxing, I must say. Therese coloured and they watched the local news and then *Jeopardy!* in easy silence.

Eventually there was the sound of footsteps on the porch and a knock at the door and Therese said that's herself there now as the door opened and Ruth's voice called in for Marthe.

Thank you for dinner, Marthe said.

Oh anytime, my love.

Marthe went out to meet Ruth, who was alone on the porch. She was feeling irritated all over again with Ruth's sudden lassitude but then saw that she was looking diminished still and just sighed. Let's go for a walk, Marthe said.

They walked along the road toward town instead of heading back to Trish's, and finally Marthe said is everything okay, is something wrong?

No, why? Ruth said.

I don't know, it seems like there is.

Nothing wrong. I got a few things on my mind, stuff to figure out, that's all. Nothing to do with you or us here.

It was getting dark but Marthe could still see that Ruth's face was bare. No eyeliner, no lipstick. It took her a minute to identify what was different.

How's the new woman then, Ruth said.

Therese? I like her. I feel like there's a person I know somehow.

Mmm.

Ruth was silent for a moment then and when she spoke again her tone had changed. Now she was going to tell a story. Marthe recognized the particular curve in her voice. Marthe knew her part to play and she let Ruth go on because she liked to go to those stories, she liked to let her lead.

John came back here looking for me once, Ruth said. The husband. He was all pissed off with Trish, she was someone to blame, like she'd lured me away.

Marthe felt a pang of something trying to imagine someone coming looking for her like that. She knew she'd likely feel differently in the actual situation, but still sometimes she wondered.

What happened? Marthe said.

Oh, he stormed around for a day or two and then he went on again. But he beat the window out of Trish's truck first.

Jesus.

Ruth waved a hand. Dramatic little shit. He was loaded, of course.

Then her voice downshifted again into the private tone that made Marthe feel like the chosen confidante.

Never think of this stuff till I'm out here again. That was the first time in my life I think I really didn't care what anyone else was doing. I barely left the house. I'd get up and get dressed and everything and then sit around in my boots all day. I had these gorgeous cowboy boots.

It was quiet out on the road, and dark. Marthe thought about walking home late at night as a teenager, drunk and giggling, nobody was ever out, the town so deeply asleep.

Ruth in this mode, telling stories, let Marthe relax. Maybe it would be okay.

30.

The days were so wide open. Marthe didn't really know what to do with herself. Trish and Therese were constantly on the go, running errands, picking up something for someone, heading over to the garden, dropping in on someone else. Ruth reverted back to bending over a cup of tea. Marthe tried to step lightly around her. She mostly ignored her phone. She wondered how this was going to work, money-wise. She had a tiny bit saved and she wasn't spending much, but there was also nothing coming in. And then she'd forget about it again. There was a familial rhythm. Sitting down to eat Trish's suppers. Marthe kept an awed distance from her. She kept a nervous distance from anything in town, anything that might have her running into anyone her own age. That would bring her back into the world. She waited for Ruth to wake back up. She went for long walks along the shore, she read all the gooey Isabel Allende novels on the shelf at Therese's place, she went to bed early beneath the yellow-flowered comforter. Sometimes when she couldn't sleep, she sat out back of the house and smoked Ruth's cigarettes. Her mind felt blank. She told herself it was okay, she just had to readjust her expectations. Sitting on the little yellow bed staring at herself in the mirror.

31

Trish said one morning at breakfast about Jenny coming next week and was that going to be an issue. Pointedly, at Ruth. No, it was not going to be an issue, Ruth said. All right then, Trish said.

Marthe asked what Jenny's last name was and typed it into her phone that night, huddled in bed. She could only get a weak signal in one corner of the bedroom, but it was enough to learn that Jenny had gone on to make documentary films. Shorts, mostly. One feature-length. Photos showed a petite woman, dark curls threaded with silver, pretty in an assertive way, a series of soft, black New York outfits, a subtle polish.

What does she do up here? Marthe asked Therese as they did the dishes the next night.

Oh, she comes up to get away, I suppose, Therese said. She has a place, her aunt and uncle's house. She visits with Trish, she works, I guess.

Marthe tried with Ruth then.

So, Jenny. You guys weren't close, or?

Oh, close, I don't know. We're a bit chalk and cheese, you know, Ruth said. It was all talk with her, all theory and books and stuff. Me and Trish just wanted to do our work, you know.

Marthe smiled at the territorial me and Trish.

I mean, I read all the books she dragged up here too, years ago. All the stuff Trish wasn't going to touch. Ruth shrugged. She was always going on about making a film, but can you imagine Trish going for that?

Marthe was piecing together a little picture of Jenny, an irritating one, out of loyalty. Jenny was one of those people who could unselfconsciously belong.

Anyway, Ruth said. Listen, I got us a little gig for the next few months. Looking after a few houses, summer home places that get rented out. We'll do the laundry and clean, get the place ready again between guests.

Okay, Marthe said. How'd you rig that up?

Oh, I still know everyone here, Ruth said. First place to-morrow.

Marthe went up to bed. Ruth and Trish were murmuring together downstairs. Marthe couldn't figure out their dynamic. She took it in out of the corner of her eye. Ruth's posture wasn't Ruth's, she had realized early on. It was Trish's. They both stood unusually upright. They never ducked their heads or slumped their shoulders like some tall women do. Ruth was more performative in her gestures, but they were Trish's. Marthe was still avoiding being alone with Trish. She didn't know how to act, she couldn't see a way in with her. Ruth needed an audience and Marthe knew how to do that, she could be the accomplice. Trish seemed like the pure, hard core of something Marthe didn't quite know how to look at directly. She gravitated to Therese instead, that sturdy openness. Therese had worked at a fish plant down the south coast for years, Therese had been a union rep, Therese had a husband go up to Alberta and never come home out of it. Her sons were easy, Mom and her partner, they said. In town, they said "friend." Therese wasn't bothered by much. She made Jiggs dinner on Sundays and she went home to watch her shows at night and she laughed and sighed and tutted on the telephone and she went out and got her roots touched up and she went to Mass on Sundays. Life was hard enough, Therese said. Marthe was at ease. Trish, tall and taciturn and always in motion, was a different story.

32.

The vacation rentals were refurbished saltboxes in bright pinks and greens and yellows. Marthe and Ruth changed sheets and scrubbed bathtubs, never seeing the tourists who came through, just the traces they left behind. Wine bottles, beer from the new brewery in the next town. Wastebaskets of tissues and condom wrappers. Pamphlets about birdwatching and whale watching and iceberg tours. Stray tea bags and soy milk containers. Marthe boiled down this detritus to two main types of tourists: young townie couples on little bay weekend getaways, and retired boomers with pensions who'd come down from the mainland or the States, the kind who could afford to go on actual two-week holidays with rented cars and the whole bit. Sometimes she would make up little stories for Ruth based on the evidence they found: This was clearly a couple, but look, they must have had a racket because I think missus slept in here, this bed is mussed and she left her necklace.

Back at Trish's, Marthe wandered the bedrooms the same way. Trish was out somewhere and Ruth had gone to the grocery store, slightly taken aback when Marthe said she wouldn't come along, pleading a headache. It was the first time she'd been alone in the house. Trish had the far bedroom upstairs, at the end of the little hallway along the stairwell. Marthe went in, listening for a car on the gravel driveway. A tall, dark dresser and matching wardrobe. A high bed. Almost no ornamentation. One framed photo on the dresser. Trish's mother and father, she assumed. A tall young woman with the same shoulders as Trish, the same thick brows, but a darker complexion. The man was visibly older than her, paler and fair. The woman was sitting, the man standing behind her, but you could tell that were they to stand side by side, she'd match him in stature. It was a small, cheap frame, a four-by-six print. The wardrobe held dresses that were clearly not Trish's. There was another row of hooks up here with Trish's shirts hung on them. A cardigan folded over a high-backed wooden chair in the corner that smelled of Therese, a pair of little gold hoop earrings on the night table.

Ruth's bed was hastily made. Her things were strewn across the dresser in her room, which had a lower, creakier double bed. Perfume, a hairbrush, loose jewellery and a lighter. Ruth was so good at taking up space in this particular way. Marthe didn't know how else to put it. Ruth could perform her femininity in a way Marthe had always felt cowed by herself. Ruth knew how to armour herself. She knew how to wear a dark red lip. Her room smelled like a smoker's clothes, like perfume and hair products. Marthe went back into Trish's room and sat on the bed. It was colder in there, and the air smelled of it. It smelled of chill and the sharp edge of bar soap and strong laundry detergent.

Ruth came back from the store and called up to Marthe about a cup of tea. She still set the pace, even though it was slower now. Marthe would say to herself sometimes that she should put her foot down, that she should go off on her own for a walk or write in her journal or read a book or call someone, but then Ruth was always there, and they had to run here or do this, even if they were going to sit down and read after supper it had to be announced and decided.

One day a bright young bearded guy came up the driveway and asked Ruth, who was out smoking on the steps, if she had a minute. He was organizing a fundraiser for the summer programming at the theatre and wondered if she would be interested in performing. Marthe, perched on the step below, watched Ruth's face. She didn't look surprised. Marthe kept forgetting how Ruth was known, or had been known. Her presence in town, upon their arrival, had been noted, even though she avoided anything remotely social.

Ruth didn't look surprised and she wasn't overly solicitous about refusing either. I haven't performed in years, my darling, she said to the guy.

All right then, well, thanks anyway, and hope to see you out at the show either way, he said, still bright, deferential.

Why don't you do it? Marthe said when he'd gone.

I have other places to put my energy now, Ruth said. I think we should get more of a plan in place, think ahead to the next couple months, she said. Jenny will be coming up and everything will go all haywire, too many people around. I'll talk to Trish tonight.

Maybe you should go down, Ruth said then. To the

fundraiser. Meet some of the young crowd. Like skipper there.

He was like twenty-two, Marthe said. She wanted to go back to talking about the plan. About Jane. She wanted to get Ruth back there at last. Marthe kept finding herself just wandering around the house. She thought maybe if they sat down all three of them that night. And then Trish wasn't home that night, she had a young client down the shore go into labour and she and Therese left in the middle of supper and there was no time to talk. Ruth seemed more irritated than Marthe. Now, suddenly, she wanted action. Marthe assumed it had to do with beating Jenny to some punch, but didn't ask. They cleaned up the supper dishes and sat reading on the front steps, huddled in sweaters.

33.

Marthe had some practical questions still. There had been no details. She hovered in the doorway as Ruth scrubbed the bathtub at one of the rental houses. How exactly did Trish perform the procedure, where did she get her, well, supplies, how demedicalized was this whole thing? And weren't the midwives regulated now, or not yet, or how did it all work exactly? Marthe knew that it was a simple procedure, she knew from her obsessive research phase that it just took someone who knew what to do, but there was still equipment to think of, drugs.

She's always had her sources, Ruth said vaguely, rinsing out the tub. The doctor back in the day, like I told you. On the sly, of course. And also, people don't get too close, but they are attached somehow, if they've come into contact with her. They think she's a bit magic or something. They want to give her things in return.

Marthe asked Therese too. Yes, there was no legislation in the province yet, but there were still a few midwives left around. You just had to go looking for it, and it wasn't free. Trish travelled to see most of her clients, when she had them. And if new laws passed, she likely wouldn't be grandfathered in; she had no papers or certification or anything, so they'd just have to see. Therese did not see Trish going in for any qualifications, but they'd be stupid to lose her. It's a good thing, I suppose, Therese said, if they get a whole system in place, but the trouble then is that it's all got to be their way.

34.

Jenny's arrival. Her step light on the front porch. She looked much like the photos Marthe had seen online. She was warm and forward, she had a soft, low voice. American, Marthe remembered. Right. Newfoundlanders had the reputation for being friendly, but really they held their guard up a bit longer, sized you up first. Jenny was a few years older than Ruth and looked at once younger and older. She looked like someone who hadn't lost any years to boozy rough patches, she looked like someone who did yoga, but she also carried herself with something older than Ruth's energy, which might have been at a simmer, but still had a kind of edge.

Jenny wasn't hesitant with the two proud, tall women.

She threw her arms around Trish, kissed her cheek. She touched Ruth's arm, she said nice to see you, so glad our time here overlapped. She hugged Therese too and then came straight for Marthe with wide, curious eyes. Oh, how wonderful, she said to Therese's introduction, that Marthe had come down with Ruth for the summer and maybe longer even, they'd see. Ruth hung back, nodding.

Jenny went down to her place and settled in and came back up for supper. She had brought wine, she had stopped for cheese before crossing the border. She drove a smart little Jeep. She talked and talked: The situation in the U.S., I mean, I think once a day about just driving up here for good, but. We can't all just run away, right?

They all mostly nodded at her, but she didn't need much more. She got away with it though, Marthe could see that. What was astonishing was the soft reception from Trish, who nodded and laughed, who made a stuffed salmon, cut big slices of Therese's carrot cake. Trish relaxed where Ruth was stiff, a sulky teenager drinking too much wine.

Late that night, Trish and Therese gone up to bed, Jenny gone home over the road. The softness suffusing Trish had lingered all evening. Marthe had watched her whisper something in Therese's ear as they did the dishes. Therese's low giggle, dishwater all over her blouse. Marthe watching Ruth remark this, their couple, the private things between them. Jenny saying good night, her mouth black with wine, wide-eyed slurring slightly how next time she would cook. Winking. Grasping their hands. Bracelets clinking on her wrists. Marthe and Ruth sat out on the step the way you do when you're escaping a party. They finished off the wine and started in on the whiskey. Marthe felt a rush of loyalty toward Ruth, she felt companionable. She had expected Ruth to be sullen still, irritated, but she wasn't. She was suddenly present again, now that the others were gone, she was relaxed, daydreaming Jane for them aloud. Marthe was continually scrambling to recast the roles played by Jenny and Ruth here, which was the prodigal daughter and which the self-righteous keeper of the hearth.

35.

Marthe was hungover when Ruth came in to get her up for work the next morning. Ruth came in with Advil and a glass of water and told her to be downstairs in fifteen minutes. They'd walk over, Ruth said, that would wake her up. The first house was a new one on their list. The owners spent one month there every July and otherwise rented it out for short-term stays only. It had been built new only a few years ago, set off from the town a little at the other end of the harbour, looking out over the water through enormous windows in the front. Marthe was taken aback when she first saw it. Oh, the Mount Pearl mansion, Therese had said, sniffing. The furnishings said money rather than taste. Marthe and Ruth wiped down counters, swept floors, washed sheets and remade beds. They wiped dust from the tops of framed photo prints of blue-green icebergs and weather-beaten saltboxes and abandoned dories and little baskets of berries. They spoke little. Marthe's head was splitting and Ruth was in work mode, insisting on checking Marthe's tasks, had she really scrubbed the tub? But Marthe felt happy, the dinner with Jenny, the table full of women the night before, and Ruth less sullen than expected, this was more like what she'd come for. Ruth checked the bathroom and then said look, you run over to the house and get the car and I'll finish up here and take you for lunch before the next place. We'll go get a plate of chips, straighten you out. If Trish is home, tell her to come along too, she's been off with missus all the time lately.

Marthe ran down the road and let herself into the house to grab the keys and paused in the porch when she heard the tenor of the voices in the kitchen. She paused and she peeked around the doorframe and she saw Trish sitting in the middle of the room, a pink towel around her shoulders, her hair wet and combed up into a peak. Therese was in one of Trish's T-shirts, fussing around her with a pair of scissors in her hand, a flirtatious edge on her laughter. Trish playing aggrieved, indignant. The chair sat on old flyers spread out over the linoleum to catch the wet curls of grey. Therese bent down, her face close to Trish's, combing the hair down straight, sizing up the length at both temples, and Marthe watched Trish reach up and take the scissors out of Therese's hands, pull her down onto her lap, those same soft, worn jeans. Therese protesting and then giving in, tucking her face into the nape of Trish's neck as Trish's hands moved over her back, pulling her in closer, one hand sliding up into her hair. Marthe grabbed the keys off the hook in the porch as quietly as possible and let herself back out. She drove over to the big house and told Ruth that Trish wasn't home.

They drove to the takeout and got cod nuggets and onion rings and cans of pop, Marthe suddenly starving, and then they drove back out to the lookout point and sat eating in the car. Ruth was relaxed, and chatty, she was speculating about the family that owned the garish house they'd just cleaned: I heard buddy frigs around on her but then I heard from someone else that she was no saint herself so I suppose it's just about the youngsters at this point or maybe they've got some kind of arrangement. Marthe sucked down her tin of drink.

Hey, how long did you sublet your place for anyway? Marthe asked then, realizing she was losing track of the days of the week.

What? I didn't.

You're still paying rent?

No, I had to give it up. I was broke.

Marthe started wiping her greasy fingers on her jeans.

You didn't tell me any of this. Where's all your stuff? When did this happen?

It's in storage, wasn't a big deal. Mind if I just smoke out the window, I don't want to get out.

Marthe nodded and Ruth rolled down the window.

So, is that why you wanted to come home? Like, for a place to crash?

Well, I won't say it wasn't one of the motivations.

Marthe took this in, her stomach turning as she picked at the glistening batter on the last piece of cod. This whole thing was just an excuse to come home then, she said. Ruth looked over at her.

But I didn't bring you down here for that. I mean, I could have just come myself if I wanted to.

Right.

I have before.

Right.

What?

Nothing, I'm just, I'm still hungover, that's all.

But later she tried to bring it up again. Trish had gone up to bed early after supper and Ruth and Marthe were cleaning up the kitchen.

So, about the end of the summer then, she said.

Yeah?

Well, are we staying on here?

Ruth said well, I mean you need to decide for yourself, I think, if you're staying or not. She passed Marthe a dishtowel and turned on the faucet.

I've got a line on a job up in Labrador for a few months, been talking to an old friend who goes up to work at this hunting lodge. So I might do that come fall. Ruth shrugged.

Marthe never able to react right away. She accepted a pot from Ruth and just stood there holding it. The lease is coming up on my apartment, she said finally.

Nothing's definite yet, Ruth said. And I'd be back eventually. Sure you're fine here either way.

I thought the point of this was that we did it together.

Jesus girl, we're not married. You'll learn, however long that takes, and then we'll both come and go. Trish's is a home base.

Marthe just nodded, her eyes burning. She was so well trained at not reacting, causing a fuss, that even when she wanted to it was delayed. She nodded and Ruth carried on as if nothing had happened, saying how the money up in

Labrador wasn't bad really, how she'd be able to save up a bit for once, pay off some debts.

Marthe put the last plate in the cupboard and said she was going to go take a shower. She sat on the edge of the tub wrapped in a threadbare blue towel and tried to integrate this new information into the story, visualizing it all laid out in front of her. She couldn't decide if this meant she couldn't trust Ruth or if she was just being called upon to expand in some way, hold some kind of "both, and." Maybe it was both, that Ruth had needed a place to stay and that they had a mission. But so far, there was not much happening on the mission front. So far, they were just living rent-free, supposedly waiting.

36.

Jenny came by early one evening and found Marthe alone on the step and said excellent, just the person I was looking for. She said I was going to go down to the new place and have a glass of wine and a bite, a little *cinq à sept*, right? I know how it goes in Montreal. Come with me?

Jenny had been by the house a few times, but briefly. Marthe had been watching her and Ruth dance around each other. They took different tacks. The only thing you'd notice from Ruth is that she never looked Jenny in the eye. She included her in the conversation, she referenced her, asked her thoughts, offered a cup of tea, but she never looked directly at her. Jenny's own directness failed her here. It is very hard to look someone in the eye when they refuse on their end. She was light still, resigned maybe. Marthe wondering what had happened between them and then realizing it was possible nothing had happened, just that they were only different enough to get in each other's way.

At the restaurant, Jenny greeted the girl behind the bar by name, she ordered a glass of white, she said they bring this in from Quebec and it's really not bad, maybe you know it already. The aesthetic of the restaurant was slightly confused, like some young hipsters from town had split the decorating job with their mothers. But it was charming in its way. The chalkboard menu, the servers in soft, washed-out aprons, the inevitable pictures of icebergs.

Jenny set them up intently, the wine, the bread and butter, a charcuterie plate (now that's all local, assured the girl) and then she turned to Marthe. This was a my-side-of-the-story moment, Marthe thought. Jenny wanted to make a good impression and the knowledge of that softened Marthe a little.

So, I want to know about you! Jenny, having arranged everything in front of them, now turned her full attention to Marthe.

Marthe laughed and shrugged. There's not much to tell, she said, and tried to steer the conversation back to Jenny.

So, you make films?

I try, Jenny said. You know, she said, I've been wanting to make something about Trish for years, wouldn't it be so perfect?

She paused. You came down with Ruth, so I assume you're in the know.

I am.

Right. So you can imagine, right? Trish is so particular, it could be a real personality-driven project. And it's so gorgeous here, I mean it would just make itself.

Marthe hesitated and then just nodded. Jenny stiffened.

I think certain stories should be recorded, she said. I think it's important. I know Ruth doesn't agree, but.

Well, Ruth just wants to keep it going.

Jenny laughed. Ruth isn't much of a doer herself. But that's beside the point. Look, I'm obviously not doing anything if Trish doesn't want, and she doesn't want, so. I put it aside. I've been writing.

This was in a confiding tone. Marthe shifted in her seat.

Anyway, I think this place is just wonderful.

The restaurant?

Yeah! And all of this, the whole town, all you young people back here doing things, it's just such a great energy.

All you young people, Marthe thought. She was included.

I could always just see it, though, Jenny said, sighing. Trish. You know, I wanted to make one of those films they make about men where she was the enigmatic cowboy shit-disturber. You know? It would be so satisfying.

She looked at Marthe's face, about to say something hesitant again, and hurried on.

But I know, I know. I'm not touching it. Shame, though.

Marthe drank her wine.

So I do have a theory, though, Jenny said.

A theory.

Ruth brought you down to sort of, bring you in on it all.

Marthe paused, considering.

You can tell me. Ruth might not be my biggest fan, but Trish trusts me. I play a different role, but I'm part of the family. And I can tell something's happening.

Yeah, well. They said they wanted to teach me, so that. So that someone knows.

Yeah.

Good, Jenny said.

Marthe? A hand on her shoulder. The voice, the fuller face now covered in a reddish beard, they belonged to Keith from high school. Remember? She did.

It's been years, he said. Are you home now or up on the mainland?

Oh, home for a while, she said. Then we'll see.

Cool, yeah, I'm out in town these days. Teaching. That's my son over there, my wife.

Marthe smiled over at them. She wondered how long it had taken him to find it normal to call the baby my son, his girlfriend my wife. He sounded so natural.

We just came out for a little long weekend, get out of town, you know.

Oh, nice, Marthe said, and then didn't know what else to say. She didn't introduce Jenny, who was smiling encouragingly.

Well, it's nice to see you, he said. I don't want to interrupt, just thought I'd say hi, been ages. He smiled back at Jenny and went back to his table.

Marthe generally looked at her contemporaries and felt tenderly about the way they were all aging. The grey hair and the worry lines and the jobs, the stoner boys turned science teachers, the party girls turned mothers, the ones who got into long-distance cycling after their office jobs or really into being parents or just never really got back on the rails, the sudden strangely earnest turn in their Facebook posts, their values showing, and their damage, and their badges of survival. A bit as if she bore none of these herself yet or a bit as if she did, she knew she did even if it's harder to see in yourself, the gradual accumulation. She was continually struck by the fact of the accumulation. That you wouldn't make it out of anything clean. You would move through things, phases, cities, relationships, but they all left a mark, a bruise, a scar. You would always have done that, lived there, felt that. Of course it was like that. This was the most obvious fucking thing in the world, but Marthe's experience of adulthood so far had mostly been a series of realizations about the most obvious fucking things in the world.

Jenny fixed her eyes on Marthe. She had a psychologist's gaze. I think it's good, she repeated.

Marthe nodded.

What do you want, though? Jenny said.

What did Marthe want, oh, she had no idea really. Marthe wanted to belong to something but she wanted it to be the right thing. Marthe wanted to really do something. Marthe wanted to hold some kind of new control in her hands, Marthe still wanted a kind of vengeance on her body. Marthe wanted to know whether or not she actually really wanted to come home. Marthe didn't want Karl back and she didn't want the baby they didn't have. Marthe wanted to keep accumulating. She wanted stories. She wanted to be Trish and Ruth and Therese and Jenny all at once. Marthe had a weakness for the future perfect. She wanted it to have been rich and complicated and joyful and messy and hard and she wanted it all under her belt already. Marthe was impatient but she also couldn't choose. Marthe wanted to live out all the stories at once, she didn't want to pick just one.

She shrank from Jenny's inquiries, waved her off, said about the wine, should they have another. She dawdled home afterward and shrugged at Ruth's amused questions about her night out on the town.

37.

Marthe itched for days beneath the memory of Jenny's steady gaze. She imagined responses:

Jenny says what do you want, though, and Marthe still never knows. She doesn't know if she came home because she wanted to or if she came home because Ruth wanted her to want to. She doesn't know if she feels betrayed by Ruth or if her reaction is just a sign of her own weakness somehow. She feels devoid of conviction, just sudden, impatient desire. The need to expend something.

Marthe planned an interlude, an intermission. She borrowed Ruth's car and drove into St. John's. She could do her own thing too, she'd had a life here she could step back into, she didn't need Ruth.

Marthe had moved to St. John's at eighteen to go to university, exactly as she was expected to do. When she finished high school there were two options: you moved to Alberta for a job or you moved to St. John's for school. She had done what was expected of her, but she had also been happy to. She'd been desperate to get out of her little town, to leave high school behind. It hadn't occurred to her to even try to get off the island; it hadn't seemed a real possibility. Halifax was the farthest anyone dared dream and those schools were four or five times the cost.

By the end of her time at university she had drifted downtown to a row house on a steep hill; she had discovered that there was a whole world that she'd known next to nothing about growing up hours away. There were artists there, and writers, and people putting on plays and making films and playing music every single night, Marthe had thought her whole life that all of these things only really happened elsewhere, off the island. And suddenly here was a whole world of it, and she wanted in on it. She was young enough to be unabashedly romantic about it all, the dilapidated yellow row house with its leaky roof, the late nights traipsing up the hill loud and loaded drunk. She would walk along Harvey Road on late winter nights and hit the fence past the Anglican church where there was a clear view of the Southside Hills and the harbour and there would be the sound of the snow crunching underfoot and she would stop and relish it every time. She finished an arts degree and went full-time at her waitressing job, and she spent the afternoons before her shifts hanging out in the coffee shop or walking along the harbour or around Quidi Vidi Lake. After work she'd ball up her greasy uniform into a tote bag and go to whatever bar the show was at that night, find her friends in the crowd. None of the different little scenes—

the film world, the theatre crowd, the art people, the writers—was big enough to exist independently or have any real gatekeeping and so she hung around the fringes of all of them, wondering what she could make. She drank too much and woke up vibrating with anxiety and only hazily made the connection between the two. Everyone drank too much, she had no real perspective on what too much was. She wrote down half-formed ideas and vague notes for projects in a little notebook and didn't have the guts to do anything with them, but she could still be involved, feel a part of things.

She had been twenty-two and twenty-three and there was this excitement, everything was thrilling, everything was possible and new. Everyone around her was burning with it too, they were so hungry, they were shrieking at each other in bars and on sidewalks, they were dreaming up projects: let's write a play together, let's make a film. Marthe was suddenly driving the van to a film shoot, working the door at the show.

The nights were seamless and expansive. Marthe was never at home, nobody was ever at home. She would leave the restaurant after a shift and hear her name called from a second-storey window, come up for a drink, come down to the show. She would sit out on her front step in the late morning and a little crowd would straggle by, we're going for breakfast at the Ship, come too. They all had phones but barely used them, Marthe would know where and when to run into the people she wanted to run into. Nobody was ever at home and there was always a next location, we're drinking in the studio, we're going down to CBTGs, come here for the after-party. They were calling a taxi at five in the morning to deliver a bottle of vodka and another of warm 7-Up; they were dancing in some painter's studio, yelling about the music. They were always drunk. They were going to a play at the Hall and then drinks somewhere and then a show and then the after-party and they were all sleeping with each other and then gossiping about it and they were busily romanticizing the whole thing to themselves as it played out, dramatic and deadly earnest, and the particularities of the place itself making it feel all the more special. There was something about having stayed, something about doing it there, in this small town of a city where everyone knew everyone, where you were still cut off from the mainland, the wider world. Marthe had believed there was something about the place itself. This place, they would say to each other, shaking their heads but secretly pleased with themselves. Marthe lying in bed hungover on a Sunday morning next to some guy, listening to the bells of the Anglican church pealing around the corner and a man standing somewhere below her window shouting over them: Go on, go on, file in, be absolved, you sinful sons of bitches, go on.

Marthe had rarely thought about any of this in Montreal. She did sometimes miss something, in those first winter months away, but she couldn't articulate exactly what.

At some point her people had started leaving. They went out west or they went to grad school or they went to teach English in Korea. Her world shrank to the restaurant and the bars open after hours. She worked double shifts, she could never get the rank smell of stale grease out of her nose, she got blind drunk in shitty little bars after work, she walked the streets drinking coffee the next day until it was time for her shift. She almost never left the tiny radius of downtown, even as it was suffocating.

The low points, when they came, were anti-climatic, almost mundane; they didn't serve as any kind of catalyst. A night Marthe found herself drinking warm vodka out of a mug in a filthy kitchen as a drunk photographer with flushed pink cheeks cut lines of shitty cocaine on the table and explained to Marthe that the guy she had been hoping to run into that night was too good for her, couldn't she see that he would never really be with her, that Marthe had just been around, a way to pass the time. Marthe had swallowed the vodka and briefly wondered if this man wanted to fuck her or the guy she was hung up on, maybe both, and nodded as he continued to explain that she was trash and she should just accept it. She nodded and nodded and just gave in, let it happen, let him beat her down so small that she felt that of course this was all she deserved, choking down her repulsion at his shiny face so close to hers. She woke up on his couch the next morning to him with hands soft on her suddenly now, cooing in some sickly sweet voice that they should go upstairs to the real bed, as if the previous night had been some kind of romantic adventure they would chuckle over later. Marthe had gotten up and walked home and showered and drank a Gatorade on her way to work another double shift, and then gone straight back out to the bar again that night.

And meanwhile the city had been changing around her. There was real money suddenly, oil money, and there was a frantic push for tourists and it worked, and they were suddenly everywhere. They were walking down Water Street in full rain gear, they were at the restaurant asking what they should do in Bonavista for the weekend and where her accent was, and she could hear her co-workers playing into it, playing it up, pocketing the tips that were a reward for the performance. Marthe would go out after work and get a few drinks in and start ranting about it, the play-acting, the pageantry, and her friends would say why are you getting so riled up about this, who gives a fuck? But she couldn't let it go.

A friend who had moved to Halifax for art school had convinced Marthe to visit, and she spent a long weekend marvelling at the little life Julie had made there. The brightly painted apartment in the North End, a tall film student roommate with rockabilly bangs, shows where people sat quietly on the floor of a gallery to earnestly listen to the band instead of getting loaded and dancing and shouting over the music. Julie and Marthe made huge breakfasts in the sunny kitchen; they smoked a joint and went thrift shopping and came home and dressed up in their new finds and sat out on the porch on a sagging couch and sipped beers as the sun went down and a gaggle of kids rode their bikes up and down the road. Marthe couldn't let herself enjoy it fully without scoffing a little at what felt like a tamer, tidier city, but she left again reluctantly.

She got on the plane to fly home and everyone's little

screen played a colour-saturated tourism commercial about how time just moves a little differently in Newfoundland, and Marthe felt like she could already smell the dank grease of the restaurant again, and she'd thought about how Julie had just started over, how she seemed to fit there now, how she looked happy and calm and had made a life where she didn't have to care ever again what anyone in St. John's was doing or what anyone in St. John's thought of her. Marthe had decided on Montreal, moved out of her little bachelor apartment into a cheaper roommate situation, stayed out of the bars and saved her tips instead, and three months later she got on the plane.

Marthe knew already that the city she was coming back to wasn't the one she'd stormed out of. It had moved on. The people she used to drink with had grown up enough to start opening cafés and bars and restaurants and vintage shops and graphic design firms, and the province was still riding a wave of good fortune, so these places were third-wave cafés with Scandinavian aesthetics, oyster bars and microbreweries. The festivals were now run by her contemporaries and they brought in young, relevant artists and musicians and dancers and filmmakers from elsewhere. The rubber boots and cartoon caricatures were scarcer, or at least relegated to the still-obligatory dinner theatres out around the bay.

But Marthe knew she could count on the late night, that vein of particular energy to tap into. She felt like acting out and she knew there was still a place for that.

38

Julie was back in St. John's now. Marthe had texted her before getting on the road. She drove up to a blue row house on Patrick Street and Julie was at the door already, admonishing a bulldog at her feet. Marthe had been apprehensive about getting in touch with anyone. She couldn't say what she was doing out at Trish's, she didn't know how to explain her presence. In the end, she tied it to Karl. She and Julie walked down the hill and over to the Duke for fish and chips, she told Julie about Karl's departure, about leaving school, and then just vaguely alluded to spending a couple weeks out around the bay for a rest, and Julie didn't press. It was a good enough story.

But how are you? Marthe said, once they'd settled into a table at the back of the bar. You seem good.

I feel good, Julie said. I was worried about coming back, but it's different now. It's been nice here, it really has.

But then Marthe said so what's all the news, and Julie launched into it. Who was fucking around on who, whose marriage fell apart six months in, who ripped off a bunch of money from the b'ys and took off with it, who got their act together for a while but then got back on the booze and got into a racket and might be brought up on charges now, we'll see I suppose. Marthe started to feel a little sick. She didn't want to know any of this, she didn't want to go back to walking around knowing these things and pretending to people's faces that she didn't, knowing they knew about her too.

Julie said anyway, I stay out of all that kind of mess now, and Marthe just nodded again.

But speaking of, Julie said with a little half smile. Have you talked to himself, or are you not going to go there?

Marthe shrugged. I haven't made up my mind yet, she said, knowing full well she was going to text him, just to see.

Julie said well he's around. She said you're going to have to be on your own tonight if you go out anyway, I have a work thing in the morning, I have to be good. But you should go out, see everyone, there'll be people on the go.

Marthe nodded, set down her empty pint glass, considering this. They settled up and hugged in the lane and then Julie skipped up the steps.

Marthe wandered the streets for a while, noting the changes. The shinier new storefronts, the awful new hotels. She thought about a neon sign she'd seen in the gallery at the Rooms once, in which the *Have* was always lit and the *Not* blinked on and off. She saw a crowd in the lane outside the Ship and went up the steps and into the bar just as a show was starting, and she drank two pints fast, standing at the bar. The crowd was younger, new. She didn't recognize a lot of them, she stood apart, eavesdropping, alert.

Now b'ys. I thought you were off the smokes. You should have seen us last night. I told her that guy's a fucking skeet. So then she said to him go on then, if you wants to go, go on, go up to Toronto and fuck that Jessica girl, I don't even care.

The put-on and the unconscious mingled. Marthe was shy and watchful and then she was drunk and effusive and the familiar faces appeared and she was hugging everyone, yes home for a while, yes nothing like it, oh I might even stay, I don't know, maybe it's time? And they would all say yes girl, Jesus, come home out of it already. It's been fun here, things are good here, sure you know now it can't be the same up there. Except for the few who were halfway out the door themselves who'd stare at her: What. Why.

Marthe fell quickly back into her old habits, old postures. Her head flicking toward the red door every time it opened. Then her phone buzzed and she walked down the steps in the lane and down Water Street and he was standing on the sidewalk, smoking. I never come here anymore, he said when he saw her approaching. But seeing who you are and all. Marthe could count on him to play the role, have the lines ready. To pick back up his part of the sloppy rhythm they'd fallen into and out of before she left. They turned into the alley and went up the stairs into the bar. Marthe, coiled and febrile. He ordered two beers and two shots of bourbon and she climbed up onto the barstool, knees spread wide. You're back, he said. Sort of, not really, Marthe said. It was still early for this place, there were just two old drunks in the bar, the bartender, them. He cocked his head and stared at her, performative, always so performative, but she had room for it, she didn't laugh, or no, she laughed, but she didn't care. Marthe only ever cringed at half-hearted dirty talk, when someone didn't lean into their part. He reached over and pushed his thumb into her mouth, still staring intently, pressing down on her bottom teeth, her tongue. His skin tasted dirty, metallic. She watched him. He said my living situation right now is not. But there is a place. Okay, she said.

He had keys to a friend's studio. There was a couch, one

high tiny window. A pipe running overhead. It was kind of a shithole. She walked to the centre of the room and reached up to grab the pipe in both hands and looked at him, bratty expectant. Okay, he said, okay. Her cheek, then, the sudden bright red sting, he never did hold back. Okay? Yeah. Good. Marthe exhaled sharp and long. Yeah, good.

The actual fucking was quick, meat and potatoes sex, once they danced around it long enough, once he'd brandished his belt, told her to shut up, to shut the fuck up giggling. They lay on the couch for a while afterward, Marthe giggling freely then, and when she made a move toward her clothes, he said we can stay over, want to stay? They had rarely spent the whole night together before, it had always been stolen time, a stop on the way home, often on the sly, they would run into each other at the bar late at night, Marthe just off work and him just finished some gig somewhere. Okay, she said, and she lay back down and he pulled a scratchy wool blanket over them.

Marthe had passed out quickly but then woke up when the first thin light came through the little window. She could never sleep after she'd been drinking. She lay there without looking over at him, shyness starting to flood through her. Their pattern used to be that they'd never make plans. She hadn't had his phone number. Maybe if she was back, maybe it would be different. Maybe they had both changed, softened in ways, gotten older. There were flecks of grey in his stubble now, his lanky body had filled out a little.

He stirred then, he woke up and leaned over her and said good morning in this soft voice she didn't recognize, he said how beautiful, her eyes, and she started to squirm, panic at his tone. But then he went on, practically crooning now, beautiful, yes, just like two piss holes in the snow. And she laughed then, relieved, she got up and got dressed and she kissed him, nice seeing you, and she slipped out quickly.

Marthe stopped at a new coffee shop, splashed water on her face in the bathroom and got one to go, and then she walked over to Julie's and got the car and drove up Signal Hill to sit and drink her coffee alongside half a dozen other people doing the same thing. She watched the other cars pulling in and out, people standing on the low stone wall for pictures, the wind whipping their hair back. Couples on an early morning together, couples with tense and tired faces, the drive a peace offering after a racket. Here, come on, let's go for a drive. Hungover friends giggling. Tourists unabashed. Lonely people on their usual rounds and solitudinous people on their usual rounds. The stupid gorgeous city with its little narrow-mouthed harbour and its bloody chain restaurants on the waterfront and the kept-up row houses and the ugly suburbs up behind the mall that nobody ever took photos of. Marthe had wanted this fiercely. She had wanted to be part of it, wanted it to be hers. She could still reach for the shreds of that spell now, but she could never quite grasp it again; it wasn't the same, it would never be the same.

She turned the car around so that she was looking out over the water instead, wondered what they were up to at

Trish's. If she was missing something. She drank her coffee and then she drove back down the shore.

Back at Trish's, Ruth said well now, how was your night? She said conjugal visit, was it? She said are you ready to get back to work now? Marthe said yes.

PART III

39.

MARTHE ANSWERED TEXTS AND EMAILS ON HER
phone at night in bed. She had been avoiding it, not knowing how she would explain herself, what she was doing at
home. But it turned out she didn't really need to explain
herself. Nobody was insistent, there were no burning questions. She was young and unattached enough that an im-
pulsive sojourn elsewhere wasn't suspect; she hung around
the fringes of enough artistic social circles that she could
get away with vague gestures at a "project" if necessary.
Marthe amused herself with the idea, as if she'd have the
gall. To be one of those people who breeze in from elsewhere for a month or two and decide to make a project,
you know, "with the community," the picturesquely struggling town. The gall of it. She would never. This was different, of course, what she was doing here.

Just taking some time at home, she wrote back. Sorry so
slow, not much screen time lately. She ignored the parts of
messages that hinted at visiting or putting them in touch
with so-and-so at an artist residency she knew nothing

about on the other side of the island, she put the phone away in a drawer.

40.

Ruth dropped Marthe off after work saying something about errands and Marthe went into the house to find Therese leaving at a clip, indignant. Talking to herself. Did you ever see the like, she muttered. You'd think it grew on bloody trees. Trish at the kitchen table with bills and a chequebook and the sullen look of someone who isn't sure they picked the right hill to die on. Marthe backing out of the kitchen then.

I don't bite, Trish said.

Marthe pausing, pulling out a chair from the table.

Therese thinks I should have more sense, Trish said.

Oh, Marthe said.

About giving herself any more help. Money.

Trish looked straight at Marthe.

She thinks I'm too soft with her. Therese had boys. You know now she didn't run a tight ship. And Jenny is after me again with this business about the movie.

Oh, the movie, Marthe said, unsure of how much she should let on that she knew.

What do you think she comes up here for? She's always at me, trying to coax me into letting her make a movie.

About the work.

Oh, I suppose. I never entertained it long enough for her to really tell me.

But wouldn't that.

Put an end to it all. Effectively, yes.

Then I kind of agree with you.

Jenny would say there is a larger point to be made.

Marthe nodded.

Not my job to make larger points, Trish said. She can find another way to do that.

Marthe nodded again, her hands still resting on the back of the kitchen chair.

Do you still want to learn?

Yes.

Ruth will make some big thing about you having to commit to stay here, but really, it's just that it might take a while, no way to predict. But then once you know, you can do what you like. Well. Not what you like, really, because then you're on the hook, if it ever comes down to it. Even if other people don't know, you'll know you have it. And you will eventually have to be here, when it's just you left, pass it on. That's all I'd ask.

But that's kind of what I want.

What.

You know. To be obliged.

Marthe cringing at her own dramatic turn of phrase and looking over to find Trish indulging it, her. Feeling the warmth of that indulgence for the first time like oh, they are all the prodigal daughters and she knows it, so stop pretending to some kind of righteousness. That's what shuts her down. Oh. Marthe sheepish at how long it had taken her to see this.

All right then.

41

All right then. Marthe would dispense with her protective sheath of irony. Her crossed arms in the corner. All right. She would try anyway.

Marthe got up before Ruth did. She rode out to the dump with Trish. Down the shore with Trish. Marthe went over to the garden with Trish every night before supper and they set lettuce and pulled weeds and shared a beer from the case Trish kept stashed in a little shrubby bush in the corner. Trish's garden was among the other narrow plots of land marked off with little riddle fences, sloping down to the shore at the edge of the town. It was potatoes and carrots and cabbages, struggling little lettuces, a bed of strawberries. Green peas curling tight over makeshift lattice. No foolishness, apart from a single tall grinning sunflower Trish would never acknowledge having planted. Trish would eventually wipe her hands and nod toward the corner and Marthe would go fetch the beer from the case and Marthe finally started asking her questions directly and she got direct responses.

It was usually uncomplicated. Early. A quick D&C, dilation and curettage. Yes, she had drugs. For the pain, for the bleeding. Sometimes she got those new pills. She had a connection. Or Jenny did, really. Yes, Jenny. Legal in France for years, sure. Then she just sat with them through the miscarriage. More unpleasant than people realized. The instruments, the sterilizer, no, it had never aroused suspicion. The midwife would have been called on for a miscarriage anyway. A few times it was too much to take on, too far along, too risky. She'd made up a story and driven the girl into the city. She couldn't be going into the clinic, though, she couldn't be seen ferrying too many. Yes, of course it used to be different, when her mother was around. Harder, yes. More desperate cases. Did Marthe know there had been a few Baptist ministers down in the States who'd been involved? Jenny had used that on the Anglican one here. No, not for himself. There'd always been a few able to see what was actually for the good. Once or twice to the hospital, yes, that was inevitable, statistically speaking. Why she kept a close eye. But no, nothing serious. They'd say miscarriage. She knew her work was good. They could maybe tell but the work was good, so. Yes, like I said, once or twice, over the years, but it was all fine in the end and my god if we're afraid all the time what would we ever get done. Do what you can when you have to. You never ever know anyway. What was the word you used the other night. Obliged. Yes, Therese was a hard one to shock. She went out to be a nurse first going off, did you know that. Never finished, but she had the stomach for it. But you can tell that.

Just wait till you've taught me, Marthe said.

Before what, Trish said. I'm not going anywhere.

Just. If Jenny, the film or whatever. Just wait till I have it and then I'll be out of sight and they can think it's in the past.

I'm in no hurry to see my own eulogy here either, Trish said.

42

Has she shown you the store yet, Ruth asked Marthe as they walked home from making beds.

No, why?

Ruth had a little grin. You'll see, she said. Missus is ready for the apocalypse.

That night at supper: So, maid, are you going to show Marthe the store or what?

Trish: Oh yes, cause I'm the funny one. You can go on and show her yourself, sure.

After supper Ruth unlocked the padlock on the red door. The store was the little white shed that stood out alongside the house. It smelled of the old cardboard lining the floor and it was orderly but completely jammed full. Gallons of water. Shelves lined with tinned food and home canning, bottled rabbit and moose and beets and jam. A deep-freeze that Marthe suspected was also full to the brim. None of which was too out of the ordinary except in the quantity. There was a lot. And then there was the other stuff. Medical supplies. Tarps. Emergency blankets.

What is all this?

It's for the storms. Or floods. She thinks storms are coming. The roads will get washed out and no supplies will get in. Or it'll be snow, or you know, some other nightmare weather scenario.

Well, I mean.

I know, I'm not saying she's totally off her head, but she didn't waste any time, god love her.

Another piece clicked into place for Marthe. Oh. Trish

was interested in a matriarchal line of knowledge, yes, but for practical reasons. It had nothing to do with making some feminist point, taking a stand. It was aligned with knowing how to grow potatoes, bottle rabbit. Trish's Jane was less the red tent and more abortion as disaster-preparedness.

Therese thinks she's nuts, of course, but you can't say anything to her about it. It's the one thing. But don't let on to Jenny that you got in here. She's dying to.

Marthe didn't bite. She was still unfurling this new understanding of Trish. Okay. Trish was looking out for the town. She wondered how many of them knew it. She imagined how Trish's house looked from the outside to teenagers in town who had heard only whispers about the strange lady who lived there. The one people talked about in secretive tones. Trish was the odd woman and the odd woman was always fodder for urban legends, for dares and jokes. Bet you won't go right on up and touch the door. Headlights slowed and bobbed and then veered off fast.

Of course nobody would know about the store, that wouldn't help matters. As it was, Trish's standing was held in delicate balance. Oh Trish, she's a bit different, you know, but she's best kind really, and my cousin thinks the sun shines out of her ass ever since she had the baby at home. Yeah. In the living room. She's a bit different, but you know. It was one of Marthe's least favourite expressions, the way people said it here. Oh I see, well that's a bit different. As in, I find that outrageous or weird or incomprehensible, but I am making a show of reserving judgment while actually judging because, you know, it takes all kinds. Life is a rich tapestry or whatever. Don't bother me one bit what people gets up to in the privacy of their own homes, but.

Marthe relished the idea a little, of the road washing out and Trish standing tall and ready. She wanted to stand tall too, a worthy heir. The only reason Marthe ever bristled at the dramatic or the overly earnest was of course because she was as guilty as they came herself.

And she would be the heir. Trish had said about the house in the garden the night before. She had turned over a bucket and sat down on it and said how if Marthe learned, if she gave her word to keep the light in the window, so to speak, the house would be hers.

It goes to Ruth first, of course. But then it will be you.

43.

Sunday night. Trish was making Jiggs. The warm starch smell of boiled potatoes. Therese hovering and then getting banished from the stove, settling in to read the flyers and provide running commentary on whatever was on sale out to Piper's. Ruth stretched out on the daybed reading. There was a knock at the door and Marthe went to open it and found a woman around her age, early thirties give or take, dirty blonde hair, soft denim maternity overalls that were sagging a little in the front, she was carrying a tiny baby. She had a gold cross around her neck, the thin chain caught up in one of the straps of the overalls. She tread gingerly as she stepped inside the kitchen.

I just thought I'd, I wanted to come by and thank you, she said, looking to Trish.

Come in, come in, Therese said. Let's have a look at him.

I've just been in town the week to see the doctor for his four weeks and he said everything is great, he's gaining weight, it's all much better.

The girl looked a little wild-eyed, though. Marthe stared at the baby. He's called Patrick, after his grandfather, the girl said, handing him to Therese, who immediately launched into furious baby talk. Who's the sweetest little treasure ever born, she demanded of the baby. Who is? Who's the sweetest little treasure?

Sit down, Trish said, here. She pulled out a chair from the table. I've got supper on, you stay now and eat something. How's he feeding?

Oh, he's best kind now. Rocky first week or so, like I was telling you, but we got it straightened out. Jeff's mom's been up, so that's been a big help.

She suddenly looked back to Marthe and Ruth, shy.

These two are down here for the summer, Therese said.

Hello, the girl nodded.

Trish said here, sit down now, this is nearly ready.

Oh, I can't stay, the girl said. I got Jeff out in the car waiting. He said to say thanks too, and he'll be up the week with some turrs he had put aside for you.

Trish just nodded at this.

And I'm sorry he was a bit. You know. She hesitated. They all thought I was nuts, but I'm glad I did things how I wanted. You know? Since you were there for Mom when I was born, and now with her gone. Anyway, she said, hearty again now, I just thought I'd bring the little feller down and show him off now he's gained a bit of weight.

Therese handed the baby back over and the girl left, calling good night, and thanks again, thanks a million.

Therese turned to Trish. You never told me you did her mother too.

Her mother was a Ryan, Trish said.

The one passed in the winter, Therese said. All right. I used to see her out to the store, my god she was some thin by the end.

Trish rounded on Marthe. We don't go repeating anything like this, when anyone comes by, you hear, she said. She married one of Gerald's crowd from over the way, and he's still convinced I talked his oldest girl into something back in the day. He had young Jeff there watching me like a hawk the whole time. Bless her heart she got her way, though.

44.

Marthe went to bed turning Trish's words over and over.

Marthe hadn't yet really thought about husbands waiting out in the car, or boyfriends hopped up on their own indignation, or suspicious fathers who never much liked Trish and what she got up to and what she got away with. Neighbours muttering about the goings on.

Marthe hasn't thought about consequences.

She hasn't thought about Jane in for questioning, Jane in the newspapers, Jane getting slaughtered on the internet. Hate mail from zealots and the cold shoulder in town.

Jane losing control of their own story.

Even now Marthe thinks about the story first, she keeps sliding away from real fear, past the threat of exposure, the resulting consequences. Marthe thinks only fleetingly about charges, a trial, her words and intentions twisted by an ambitious prosecutor, Jane called out for actually thwarting the agenda by not quietly working within the system.

Marthe leaps forward to explaining herself to a sympathetic journalist. She leaps forward to surfacing on the right side of history, Jane emerging once again triumphant. She doesn't think about the fact that Trish is old, that Therese has grandkids. She doesn't think about the fact that the narrative will entirely depend on public opinion in the moment things are brought to light. Whether there's a larger story that their little resistance can be part of. Whether sympathy will fall with them or not.

Marthe walked around alert and anxious for a few days and then fell back into the rhythm of their days and forgot to be worried, soothed by Trish's sturdy presence. Jane would be too big to buckle that easily, Jane would not be so easy to pin down. Jane could never not own their own story.

45.

Jenny just loved the young new crowd running the place now. She just loved all the new developments. My god, I remember the first time I came up here, she said to Marthe, whom she had corralled for another drink at the restaurant. I was eighteen and I'd lived in Chicago my whole life and I'd never seen anything like this place. It was a game-changer. I mean, that and everything else, Trish and everything, of course, I'm sure you know the story. But all of it. It woke me up.

Marthe shifted, trying not to feel embarrassed, the bartender clearly eavesdropping.

Anyway, it's just wonderful now that everyone recognizes it, you know, the world knows now, how it's so special here, so particular.

Marthe nodded. She had mostly given up on this argument, she had stopped taking the bait when people gushed to her at parties in Montreal about Fogo Island and St. John's and the Battery and how they'd had this cab driver, see, and how they'd gone to the Inn of Olde because they were the right kind of tourists who knew better than to go to George Street. When they gushed about their visits, Marthe blandly gushed back and told them where to go and what to do the next time, the contrarian position too exhausting to uphold. But now suddenly she couldn't help herself. Jenny was wine-drunk, dressed expensively, emphatic, embarrassing.

I don't know, it all makes me squirm a little. I don't know who a lot of this is for. And then the dancing for the tourists and the fucking Screech-ins and everything while the place is falling down around our ears most of the time.

Oh, it's all just a bit of fun, everyone knows that.

Yeah, but.

Marthe stopped. The indignation draining out of her just as quickly as it had surged up. She didn't actually care so much anymore, really. She couldn't get it up for her own spiel, it wasn't worth it, just let Jenny have it, she wasn't totally wrong, none of it was ever totally wrong, yes it was special here and even yes it was fun to slide back down into a particular rhythm of speech, lean into an accent, she did it all the time herself, she knew exactly how to wield it to get a laugh, she was no better than any of the rest of them. So let Jenny have it.

Yeah, I don't know, it just used to get on my nerves, that's all.

Well, of course, Jenny said. It makes sense you'd be protective.

Well, no. I wanted to leave, growing up. And then suddenly I wanted to stay and then I wanted to want to stay and then I just left and now I'm half jealous of what went on without me, maybe.

Jenny was of course now holding Marthe's wrist and nodding, wide-eyed, earnest.

Marthe sighed. I like it here with Trish, she's no bullshit.

Agreed, Jenny said, dropping Marthe's wrist and raising her glass.

Tell me about New York, Marthe said, letting it go, downing her own glass. When you first got there, she said.

Oh Marthe, it was just so exciting.

Jenny's optimism translated to an unflagging generosity of interpretation, Marthe had to give her that. Jenny had arrived in New York just in time to watch all the radical feminist groups disintegrate into power struggles and infighting but, she shrugged, all that's kind of inevitable.

People are loath to talk about it because they don't want to make us all sound like petty bitches and, like, hurt the cause, but some of them were petty bitches! We're just people. It's worse if we have to pretend to be saints and sisters. I mean, my god, of course people couldn't agree, there were so many conflicting ideas and directions and so many blind spots and so much stubbornness. But you know, just because it came apart eventually doesn't mean it failed. I hate it when the story is told like that. None of these things were ever meant to stay on in the same form forever.

Marthe said this is unrelated, but did you ever want to have one after? Like, a baby? Sorry, that's a weird thing to say, maybe.

Oh, I tried, Jenny said. I lost two. And then I was just too old. So there was that. I'm relieved that I didn't have that first one, but I didn't think it was going to be the only shot. We gave up.

She paused, sipped her wine. Pretty sure he went for Ruth at one point, one of the summers he came up here with me.

Who did?

Oh, James. My guy. We were never married or anything, but it was ten years, we had kind of an open-door policy, you know, but still.

So, did she?

I don't know. Never asked, don't really need to know. Ruth doesn't like me too much, but it's because we're too alike. I always knew that. I was so in awe of her back then. She would come by between tours and she was so young, but she had that presence. But we just never really clicked. I'm glad she found you. It's a good fit. You're a good fit. Feels like things can start happening here again. Some momentum. Back in the day I was always trying to bring some of that energy up here, you know. With varying degrees of success. Trish, you know. But maybe now, you're here, I don't know, I see an opportunity.

Jenny topped up their glasses, she turned wistful, ordered another bottle. Marthe asked the girl if they could have more bread. Should we eat something, maybe? she asked Jenny. She could feel the red wine staining her cheeks.

I wanted her to come down, you know, Jenny said in response. I had all these ideas, the things we could do. Everyone was talking about making new communities then. You know. Living apart. Doing it another way. Without men. Which, I know, I guess there was a bit of a hitch in our case with what were we going to need abortions for then, but you know, there was some way in which it still all kind of made sense. To me, anyway. Jenny laughed. Trish was having none of it, of course. It wasn't even a fight. She would just laugh. Didn't even entertain it. I was coming up from university, you know, there were lesbian bars, there were lesbian separatists! I mean, I get it, I suppose. She wanted to keep up the work, the midwifing, and it's a small town. But it used to rile me up. She didn't seem to feel like she was having to suppress herself or anything.

But did she, were there others?

Oh yes. I mean, I think people just saw what they wanted to see and left it alone. There was a teacher from away who came here for a while. But again, missus wanted her to move out to St. John's or somewhere even bigger, start over, and Trish wouldn't go. I think there were a few different incarnations of that story. But anyway. You just have to accept it at a certain point, right?

Marthe nodded, reaching for the bread that had been deposited on the table. She was feeling slurry now, she was stuck on Jenny's "missus," the slightly foreign sound of it in her American mouth even if Jenny had been coming here for longer than Marthe had been alive. But Jenny was barrelling on.

Same thing with your Morgentaler though, you know. What I was saying before, Jenny said, nodding at her own point, her eyes wide.

What? What about him?

You know. He was a womanizer. And it never really had to come out the way it would now, you know, the inevitable downfall of any male saviour of women pretending to sainthood. He risked so much and he did this extremely important thing and he also cheated on his wife, he slept around, whatever. Three wives, even, I think. I don't know. I'm not congratulating him on it, but I always liked that it pre-emptively prevented anyone from placing him on some mealy-mouthed untouchable holy pedestal. You know. I mean, there's a line, of course. But if it's just that you were kind of a bitch or whatever.

Jenny was full outstretched arms now, gesturing, emphatic. She was slurring her speech just slightly. She insisted they have a last drink, she ordered whiskeys, winked at Marthe. She tipped outrageously. Marthe threw up outside the bar and woke up in Jenny's guest room.

46

Jenny had inherited her aunt and uncle's place when they died a year apart. Her own parents had split when she was young and her father had been a hard person to keep track of and her mother a hard person to get along with. But the aunt and uncle were easy and kind, they knew what it was to not do what was expected of you. Jenny's mother hadn't spoken to her brother again after the draft dodge; she had remained on civil enough Christmas-card terms with his wife only to send Jenny up there when she got in trouble at college.

Jenny told Marthe all of this over breakfast. She had a little stovetop espresso maker; she'd brought up bags of beans from New York. She breezed around the kitchen in a yellow-flowered silk kimono, making omelettes, humming along to the Patsy Cline playing from her phone. Marthe tried to imagine if she'd met Jenny when she was a teenager. Jenny would have seemed of entirely another world with her clothes and her espresso and her books, her offhand mentions of London and Berlin, the filmmaking and the activism. Marthe would have fallen directly under her spell. There'd been no odd women in Marthe's town growing up, no travellers, nobody glamorous, no come from aways. She never met anyone who'd been out and come back with the smell of the world on them.

Jenny had inherited the house in the late nineties and fixed it up, bit by bit, but tastefully, of course. I wanted to preserve it rather than remodel it, you know, she said to Marthe. It still had low ceilings and the small bedrooms upstairs, but a sexy little woodstove in the middle of the living room and kitchen, which had been knocked together and opened up. It was the kind of place Marthe felt sheepish about longing for. She barely wanted to admit that she had begun, in these strange lulling weeks of housekeeping and gardening with Trish and riding around in the truck, to nurse again the fantasy of a life where she never did leave, where she and Ruth and Trish all lived together, doing the work and growing their food, and maybe Marthe would spend a few weeks here and there back in Montreal, where she would finally have some kind of important artistic work, "projects" and "collaborations" that were hazy apart from the setting up of meetings and the need to be back in the city to "touch base." Maybe they would take Jane on the road, they would appoint heirs in other remote towns, it would finally be the network she and Ruth had daydreamed of. And then in some more distant future, when it was just Marthe left, she would live in the house that would be like this one by then, touched up, fixed up just a little, and she would have the old daybed still and a few dogs and she would be the odd woman then, and the younger people would come to her to learn, and her house would be the gathering place.

Jenny had a book about Jane, the Chicago Jane. She had a book about Jane and she had countless little broadsides and pamphlets and she had shelves full of tape, she had photos. The archives got too big for my apartment, she said. Documentation is important, she said. Just think of all the stories nobody knows. Things they don't want us to remember, it breaks the line of continuity, it prevents any real progression. Marthe couldn't quite hold Jenny's eye during this little speech, but she walked home with the Jane book under her arm, lightheaded and hungover and a little dazed but relieved. Her dread about finding out what had gone down between Ruth and Jenny, her worry that these dynamics were too tense, too complicated, and how she didn't know how to be the one to rise about them, maybe it was all unnecessary! She felt almost jubilant. They could still do the work. The work would come first.

And when she, when Marthe, she decided, when Marthe years later in her own odd woman home wrote the book about their Jane, she would make that point very clear.

47.

Jenny was scarce for a few days and then she showed up with company. A woman about Marthe's age. She had thick, curly hair, a boxy blazer over a faded T-shirt.

This is Kara, Jenny said. I've just been in town to get her at the airport.

Kara appraised the kitchen, and Trish and Ruth and Marthe, as Jenny made introductions. She was all direct eye contact and firm handshake.

She's working on her PhD, down in New York. But she used to do some research and editing for me sometimes. And might again, hey?

Kara nodded, a tight smile. Marthe immediately clocked Kara as the kind of person she'd been intimidated by at grad school. Kara probably spoke in paragraphs, had orderly linear understandings of things, talked like the theory she read, made surprising connections.

Anyway, Jenny said, we haven't even made it to the house yet. Just thought I'd drop in on the way.

Marthe looked to Ruth when they'd gone. What do you think that's about?

Ruth shrugged. Maybe she's finally going to make her big film.

Jenny came back alone hours later. Kara's napping, she said.

She didn't sit. She was more tentative than usual. There was a scratchy sound to the radio, like someone had brushed the dial and knocked it just a hair off the frequency. The beginning of the long dash following ten seconds of silence indicates exactly one o'clock. There was a ragged edge on the tones.

So, Kara only called me from the airport, Jenny said, shaking her head. I didn't know she was coming. An impulse, she said, something about a breakup. And she knew I was up here, I'd been in touch, and.

And what, Ruth said.

And then she told me in the car that she's pregnant and she doesn't want to keep it. And she asked if ... See, I told her my story, a few years ago, you know, just the bare bones of it, just between she and I, we're close, and I trust her, and she's had bad experiences with doctors in the past, so I do understand her coming, you must too, right?

This all in a breathless rush.

Ruth: What?

Trish didn't speak right away, then: Well. She's after coming all this way. Seems a bit much to me, considering she was in the city and all, but.

Ruth pounced.

What does she think this is? Some hipster boutique experience? This was not the intention, some tourist attraction hippie earth mother bullshit she could buy. This was supposed to be about necessity.

Marthe stared at Ruth. Wait, what?

Trish overruled. I don't think we're in any danger of becoming a tourist attraction, Ruth. Come on now.

Ruth made a face. You know that's not what I mean. But it's a bit of a trot to come all the way up here for this. She's got money to throw around, does she?

Trish said listen, she's here now and if she wants help, I'll help her.

Jenny looked relieved. I didn't invite her up here on purpose or anything, I swear.

I know, Trish said.

But then when she asked, I did think. Well. Strange to say I thought you'd be happy, but. You've got Marthe here, and. It is what you're trying to do.

Ruth left the room.

Don't mind her, Trish said. Marthe wasn't sure if that was for Jenny's benefit or her own. She didn't know which side she was on. She was instinctively skeptical of Kara but knew she should at least try to parse out her own insecurities from any real suspicion. Mostly she was nervous. If they were going to do this thing themselves then people were going to come and have them do it. Obviously. That part just hadn't been this close yet.

Trish said tell her tomorrow. The sooner the better.

Tomorrow. Marthe felt queasy. Tomorrow. She stared at Trish, who seemed towering again now in her unafraid steadiness. Therese said all right, well, let's get organized tonight then. Ruth had gone upstairs, the door shut behind her. Marthe wished she would come back down.

Trish looked at Marthe. You can see now, see what it is from the other angle. Marthe nodded.

48.

Jenny and Kara arrived early the next morning. Jenny's face was set but Kara looked just as assured as the day before. Kara in the same blazer but with soft drawstring pants underneath, a laptop in a tote bag from the Strand. Marthe had been worried that Ruth would stay shut in her room, sulking, but she was already downstairs when Marthe came down, she was on, alert. Awake again, finally. She was not letting Jenny have this one.

Okay, Trish said. She put a hand on Kara's shoulder. She said let's just get right to it. Come up and we'll chat a bit first and then get started.

Marthe watched Ruth and Therese get up and follow before she set down her cup of tea and stood, bracing herself.

The back bedroom upstairs. Light grey and airy. The rustle of plastic beneath cotton. Marthe in her sock feet, should she go put shoes on? Therese was hostess and nurse, it was Therese showing Kara to the bed, here's a sheet to slip under, just take everything off from the waist down, my love. Kara with a look of mild annoyance at Therese's ministering. It was for that Marthe disliked her. She didn't get it, she didn't get Therese. Jenny patting hands, excusing herself, she wasn't much for this part, she'd be in the kitchen. How far along. About seven weeks. Yes. She had an app, she tracked everything. Here, look. Okay. Trish's voice in a different register now, Trish's low voice commanding the room. Ruth and Trish moving confidently through a silent, practised choreography. Kara dropping her detached look. Kara nodding. Marthe leaning in.

Ruth, gloved, beginning. Palpating. Nodding to Trish. Trish speaking low. Trish this is something we are going to do together, do you understand? Kara nodding yes. Trish here is what I am going to do first. And here is what we are going to do next. Kara looking up at Therese, Therese nodding, Therese the cool, dry hand, Therese the soothing presence. Trish this is for the pain and this is for the bleeding, but it is still not going to be pleasant. Trish now for the opening. Slowly. Kara gritted teeth, eyes on ceiling, exhaling exhaling exhaling. Trish here's what's next. Are you with me, are we good? Here's what's next, Kara. I am listening, I am feeling for a sound, a textured sound. Now. There it is. Breathe. Breathe. I know. I know. Almost there. Now. There. That's it. That's it. You can. Yes. Breathe. It's done.

Therese still in quiet action, Therese busy tidying, Trish in her place at the head of the bed now. Speaking low just for Kara. Touching her just once more, moving sweaty hair off her face. Marthe exhaling. Ruth pulling off her gloves.

Marthe felt she had experienced the last twenty minutes in two separate simultaneous streams. One was a kind of sensory overload, the acute attention of adrenaline. Every shade of colour in the room, the different notes of the scents in the air, disinfectant and the iron edge of blood. And the other was calm and straightforward because Trish was calm and straightforward. Trish was performative here, but it was a particular kind of performativity—she had assumed something with that "we." We are going to do this here today. We are both participants. It was the first time Marthe had actually witnessed a departure from the pragmatic in Trish. A moment of unselfconscious solemnity. Are you ready? Then it was calm pragmatism again, it was deft hands, it was a steady voice guiding a shaky one. Okay? Okay. Trish providing that same bookend Marthe had been given: You're no longer pregnant.

Marthe slipped out. She went downstairs to the kitchen and Ruth was not far behind her. Ruth pulled out a chair from the kitchen table, she looked at Marthe's shaky hands, she put on the kettle.

49.

Kara was to stay overnight. Trish said it's not absolutely necessary, but since she can, why not keep an eye on her? They had lunch and Trish fixed a tray for Kara. Marthe was delegated to bring it upstairs.

She pushed through the half-open door gently, remembering her own dazed hours, the body surprised to be so suddenly rerouted. She decided she would make an effort, she said hey, Trish sent up some lunch, how are you doing? But Kara wasn't much for chatting. She was sitting up in bed on her laptop, she thanked Marthe for the tray, she said yeah yeah I'm fine, gonna just catch up on some work here, I think. Her eyes flicked back to her laptop.

Marthe nodded and backed out of the room again. Back downstairs she reported that Kara was fine, she paced around the kitchen, she was keyed up. She couldn't sit still. Therese looked at her and said why don't you come over for the cards tonight?

The cards, Marthe said.

Yes, my card game. Few of the girls come by about once a month.

Trish?

God no. She hasn't got the patience for it.

Therese came back around for Marthe after dinner that evening. You coming then, she said, poking her head into the kitchen. I've got to run down and pick up some mix, you can come on with me now. Marthe got up from the table. You look out now, Trish said. Missus will take you for everything you've got.

That's why she won't come play, Therese said. Look of her. Too scared.

Yes now. Trish flicked a dishcloth at them. Go on then.

Therese looked to Ruth at the table. What about yourself then?

No, no, you go on, Ruth said.

All right then, just me and the young heir here, Therese said. Come on then.

Therese drove over to the convenience store and they went in for ice and Pepsi and a half case.

Having company, the woman at the store said.

At the house, Therese already had the kitchen table pulled out into the middle of the floor, extra chairs squeezed in around it. The women came in low, they were quiet, solicitous to Marthe. Oh my, isn't that lovely, they said to Therese's introduction of Marthe, home for the summer now over to Trish's. My crowd hasn't been home in years, one woman said before raising her voice to someone else at the counter mixing a drink: That one's for me, is it? They came in quiet at Marthe and then came in brash at each other. Look of herself over there, gracing us with your presence tonight then? They drank rum and cokes and Coors Light poured out into glasses, they said them little cheese things are some nice, Therese, where'd you get them? A woman called Pat, who was the secretary up at the high school and had on a full face of makeup and kept slipping outside to smoke, finally rapped on the table with the deck of cards. Now b'ys, are you just here for a gab or are we going to play cards? Marthe sat to the table obediently.

As Pat was about to deal, Jenny slipped in the kitchen door. Room for one more? she asked, winking at Marthe, who felt a twist of frustration, now Jenny was going to be there observing everything and making it clear that Marthe was too, Marthe on the outside too, when she wanted just to blend in, to not make this such a self-conscious experience. But the women seemed to know Jenny. Oh, I was right in the mood to win some of those nice American dollars, one of them crowed, and Jenny said, no, no, I learned my lesson last time when you took me for all I had. I'm ready to turn the tables now. She winked at Marthe again and swigged from the beer Therese had passed her. Marthe cringed at her one of the girls tone.

They played hand after hand and Jenny lost terribly and one of the women looked at Marthe and said you don't find it spooky up there at the house, I finds that house some spooky, and Marthe just shook her head, uncertain. Therese waved a hand at the woman. Don't be so foolish, Wendy, for god sakes. Jenny drank beer and let the women take everything she had and let them take the piss out of her mercilessly and finally bowed out, and then someone's barrel-chested husband was at the kitchen door, now my love, are you after betting the house or what, come on, what kind of state are you in now?

When they'd all gone and Therese and Marthe were gathering up empty glasses and bottles and pushing back in the table, Marthe said why did that woman think Trish's place was spooky?

Who, Wendy? Don't mind her, she's foolish as a bag of hammers, that one.

Yeah, but is it because of the work, or?

No, no. I mean most of them have an idea of what goes on, but you know. Ask me no questions, I'll tell you no lies. They know not to give me the third degree on Trish.

So, what is it?

Oh, some old story about Trish's mother. There was a young girl who'd given it a go herself first and she showed up hemorrhaging and she never made it, never had a chance, but you can imagine the way the story got twisted.

She died, Marthe said.

Therese turned on her suddenly.

Yes, she died. And Pat there, her son fell out of the boat when he was young and he's been a bit simple ever since, and missus next door's husband got in his new truck and destroyed himself and left her with the four youngsters, and that young girl never made it and probably was never going to make it and you think some other young one didn't show up looking for help just weeks later? We just keep on. All you can do.

Okay, Marthe said.

So never you mind foolish old women with a few drinks in them.

Okay, Marthe said.

Now you want to stay on here tonight? I got clean sheets on in the blue room, you go on up to bed you wants.

50.

It was the week of the big summer festival in town, and Ruth and Marthe had their hands full. They had to get every rental house ready. Jenny would be renting out her spare room, the town readying for an influx that would nearly double its population for a few days. The town hadn't settled for some little bay festival with a country music act and Newfie night at the stadium. It was expensive. They were aiming to get people to fly in for it. There would be tents in yards, Ruth and Marthe were putting out extra sheets at the houses to make up the couches too. Therese was down at the legion helping with some dinner, Jenny was all excited, Trish was oblivious. Ruth and Marthe were just doing laundry.

Marthe hadn't seen Jenny or Kara in the days since the abortion. Jenny had picked Kara up by the time Marthe got home from Therese's the morning after, she obviously hadn't said a word about any of it at the card game. Marthe had assumed Kara would lie low for a few days at Jenny's and then be back off down to New York. But when Jenny burst into the kitchen one evening after supper, flushed and excited and chattering about the little concert at the old twine loft and a picnic dinner down the shore, and how they should come down tonight to the dance at the legion, Kara was right behind her, smiling and nodding when Jenny looked to her for an expression of shared enthusiasm.

Only Therese really indulged Jenny. Oh my, she said, that sounds lovely. I'll be off to bed out of it but maybe these younger ones will join you. She nodded at Marthe, who shook her head instinctively but smiled at Jenny apologetically. Ruth just took it all in quietly; she had been stretched out on the daybed in the kitchen and took her time sitting up when Jenny and Kara arrived.

Once they had bustled back out of the house, Jenny calling out that if they changed their minds, they'd know where to find her, Marthe felt a pang of regret, maybe she should have gone, maybe she should get over herself. Ruth lay back down and asked for the time.

Where'd they say they were going? Ruth asked then.

Down to the legion, Therese said.

Ruth nodded at this silently for a moment and then got up and went into the bathroom and came back out a few minutes later, her eye makeup reapplied. She looked to

Marthe. Let's go get the smell of the house off you, she said.

Marthe made a face. To the legion?

No, no. Steering clear of that, Ruth said. She threw on her jacket, pulling her hair out over the collar. She put her boots on and looked at Marthe. Coming?

Marthe got up then and went into the hallway for her own jacket; she stopped at the little mirror at the foot of the stairs and mussed her hair a little, pulled her shoulders back. She went back out to the kitchen and followed Ruth out the door, calling good night to Therese.

Where are we going? Marthe asked then, as she trotted alongside Ruth, trying to keep up with her long strides.

We'll go down to the bar and have a drink, Ruth said.

Oh, okay! Marthe brightened immediately.

Ruth looked sidelong at her. Doesn't take much, does it, she said.

The bar was a squat building with white siding, Christmas lights still tacked up along the eaves. Every head turned when Ruth and Marthe came through the door, but the attention they attracted shifted again just as quickly, the heads went back to their drinks or their VLTs. The woman behind the bar was around Ruth's age, and she too stared a moment before going back to what she was doing. Ruth didn't notice the acute awareness of their presence, or she affected not noticing. Marthe followed her to a couple seats at the end of the bar, and the bartender dutifully appeared in front of them moments later. How are ye tonight, she said. Oh good, good, Ruth said. They ordered beers and once the woman had set the bottles down in front of each of them, she paused a moment and said is that Ruth? The question carefully offhand, as if it had only just occurred to her, as if she hadn't recognized Ruth the minute they came through the door.

Tis, Ruth said, with an exaggerated little wink and nod. This is Marthe, she said then, indicating with her head.

Marthe smiled at the woman, who said wonderful, that's wonderful, well good to see you, been ages, and then went off back down to the other end of the bar to perch on her stool.

Marthe drank her beer and watched Ruth, whose energy had shifted. Here she was. Here was the dark eyeliner and the glittering, perceptive gaze. Ruth in her element. Two older men inched their way up toward them at the bar. It's my birthday, one of them announced. He had a Harley Davidson leather vest on, chunky rings on his fingers, a small man, still slim. His sidekick was taller, gangly limbs, a soft belly. He was drunker too, his slurry speech garbling an accent so thick he sounded almost Irish. Now b'ys, Ruth said in response. She bought a round for them all, they were clinking glasses.

You're the one what did the music, the Harley Davidson man said then, after sizing Ruth up for an obvious long moment.

Once upon a time, yes, Ruth said.

I play myself a bit, he said then, proudly.

Marthe watched Ruth carry on with the two of them, now she could notice how it was deliberate, Ruth's charm, her seductive energy, now Marthe could observe it as something she wielded. It didn't necessarily take away from the experience—Marthe was laughing and carrying on right along with them, she was happy, she hadn't been out like this in ages. But it was something she filed away quietly.

The next thing, the Harley Davidson man, Wilf, had unearthed a little button accordion from somewhere and was wondering if Ruth would have a little tune with him, and the bartender was asking them to play "Ring of Fire" for her, she loves that song, sure there's a guitar there somewhere in the back if you want, Ruth?

Ruth was gallant, she let Wilf take the lead, she strummed along with him and sang the Johnny Cash song for the bartender, and then she sang "Sonny's Dream" because a woman at the VLTs who was wrist-deep in a bag of Cheezies wandered over asking for it, and finally Wilf said okay, now you pick a tune for us, let's have one from you.

Ruth perched back up on her stool and thought for a moment and then waggled her eyebrows at Marthe and started singing, a song Marthe recognized but couldn't place at first, until she realized Ruth was winking and smiling out of the side of her mouth in the same way she had in one of the videos Marthe had found of Ruth years ago, singing this same song, a saucy little tune she belted out now, faster and faster, without missing a beat. Marthe was drunk now, she was roaring in delight, clapping her hands at Ruth as she finished with a flourish, Wilf with a bit of a pout on because he hadn't managed to keep up playing along. Did you write that, Marthe said breathlessly.

No, girl, Jesus, it's Buffy Sainte-Marie! Ruth shook her

head at Marthe, tipped back the last of her beer and said all right, that'll be our parting song here. She linked her arm in Marthe's and led her out the door.

51.

Marthe barely slept but woke up still energized the next morning. She got up, determined to get Ruth out to do something else, something nice, it was high August and they'd been inside cleaning half the summer. Ruth would not be talked into a hike, but she conceded to berry-picking. She got a couple of beef buckets from the store and led Marthe, delighted, up the hill behind the school.

They came over the curve of the hill and settled down in the clearing where it levelled off, squatting a few feet apart in the low brush.

So, Ruth said. We haven't really talked about the other day.

Yeah, Marthe said. It was real, she said.

Marthe felt flushed in the sun, high on a kind of after-glow exuberance thinking back on it, the procedure, the knowledge that she had actually done it, or at least, done the witnessing.

I was afraid I'd bail, Marthe said. That I wouldn't have the stomach when it came down to it.

I knew you did, Ruth said.

Yeah, Marthe said, smiling now. Yeah, I could do that, right. I think I could. I just had this feeling, like, okay, this could be me.

It will be you, Ruth said.

I mean I guess it will take a while, you know, to really learn, but we've got time.

Marthe chattered away, shifting so she was kneeling now over the bushes, plucking little fingerfuls of berries, popping some in her mouth. She could see it clearly finally. They were doing what they came for, Ruth was finally awake again, they would be Jane, it wouldn't be just some story they told themselves.

Well, and you know now you've got a place here. You can stay on as long as you want, Ruth said, shifting to a squat, brushing off her knees. Marthe looked up.

Ruth went on, yes, this will work out just fine. I've got a little money now to go on, I'll be able to make a nice bit up in Labrador too, that'll set me up for a while.

Marthe felt an anxious twist in her stomach. You're still going to go, she said.

Well, yeah. I never said I wasn't.

I just thought, now that things were happening here.

Trish and this place aren't going anywhere. We've been here a few months now. I'll be back at some point.

Marthe stood up. You can't just come back here when you're broke, she said.

Oh, excuse me.

No, fuck this, you're always going on about commitment and me running off and you're the one trying to fuck off out of here again the minute you get some money out of Trish.

It was hard to run down the hill and even harder to do it while carrying a bucket of blueberries and trying not to cry with rage. Marthe switched her gait and took giant, barrelling steps. Ruth had called after her once. Marthe didn't look back to see if she was following.

Marthe wait, just fucking wait.

Ruth was coming after her. The harsh edge on her voice still at first. All right, well, fuck you then, Ruth said. The nerve of it. You think you know me and Trish, you think you know everything.

Marthe crying now, pissed at herself, she could never not cry once someone started yelling, it took all the fire out of her own rebuttal.

Ruth trying a different tack then, her temper flaring out again just as quickly, her voice softening.

Marthe, wait. You're making a big deal out of nothing. It's not like I'm abandoning you on the side of the road. You're not alone here. Sure you and Trish haven't had much need of me in the last few weeks, you've been off with her half the time, doing your own thing.

They made it to the house, Marthe walking a few steps ahead, and she left her bucket on the steps and immediately turned and left again, dodging Ruth. She went out to the garden and drank the last beer in the hidden case and then she went over to Therese's and sat on the step, sulking, until Therese got home and said of course, go on up, you know you're welcome anytime.

52.

In the morning, Therese made a big breakfast and didn't ask any questions. She chattered on about what she and

Trish had gotten up to the day before, and the crowd out to the store, and the news from her son out in town, letting Marthe half listen over a second cup of tea. They were still at the table when Jenny appeared at the door, Kara in tow.

Sorry to burst in like this first thing, Jenny said. I was looking for Marthe. Trish said she'd be here. She looked at Marthe. Are you working today? Can we borrow you, maybe?

No jobs today, Marthe said.

I promised I'd go bring the chairs back down from the legion to the theatre but I double-booked myself. Could you come help out in my place? Kara will join you, it shouldn't take long.

Marthe tried to hide her frustration. When was this person going to leave? But she nodded at Jenny, she said sure, I can help. Likely Kara would be gone soon anyway, this was not a big deal, she told herself. And she didn't feel like going back home to Trish's or dealing with Ruth yet.

Marthe and Kara set off down the road soon after Jenny had rushed on out ahead of them, climbing into her Jeep calling out thank-yous to Marthe still. The silence that set in after she'd driven off stretched just long enough that Marthe wondered if they'd really just let it continue, but she couldn't manage it, and finally she said so you decided to stick around a few more days? She wondered if it sounded as effortful as it felt.

What? Oh yeah, well, I didn't have much of a plan I guess, Kara said.

Oh, Marthe said.

And yeah, it's cool here, not what I expected. Maybe I'll stick around for a while.

Marthe couldn't stop herself, she knew the face she was making, her eyebrows knit in judgment as she looked over at Kara directly finally.

What are you going to do?

Oh, I don't know. Jenny said there might be a job at the restaurant, or I could just hang out for a while. Kara shrugged. She stopped then, pulled her phone out. Hang on a second.

They were rounding the bend in the road that brought the harbour into view. The morning was grey, and misty. Kara held up her phone and took a photo, Marthe snarking to herself about how Kara would caption it when she inevitably posted it online. As if she hadn't stopped at this very bend in the road herself and snuck a photo when the light was like this or when the fog was hanging low. Kara was unselfconscious about it. She didn't care about the truck that drove past as she was holding up her phone, that the driver would see them and think they were tourists, or townies out for the weekend.

Cool, Kara said, putting her phone back in her pocket. I think we can cut up this way, actually.

I know, Marthe said.

At the legion, Kara strode through the door confidently and greeted the woman sitting at the bar. Back for the chairs, she sang out in a looser tone than Marthe had ever heard from her.

All right my love, that's fine, the woman said, and went back to her coffee.

Marthe followed stiffly as Kara got right to it, grabbing the metal folding chairs that were scattered around the perimeter of the room and stacking them against the wall by the door.

The guys from the theatre are going to come up with the truck to get these, and then we can just follow them down and help set them up, Kara said.

Help yourself to a coffee there, girls, if you like, the woman at the front called. I'll be in the office if you need me.

They stacked the last of the chairs by the door and then Kara looked at Marthe. Coffee? Marthe shrugged and said okay, sure, and watched Kara march down to the bar and pour two cups. Let's sit out front and wait, Kara said then, as she handed Marthe the coffee. She pulled out her phone. I texted the guy and he said he's on the way. He's cute, this guy, Jake or John or something, do you know him?

Marthe shook her head, not wanting to admit to Kara that she didn't know anyone here. Maybe seen him but I don't think so, she said, pretending to think about it.

Once they were sitting side by side on the wooden steps out front, Kara said so what's your deal here, anyway?

What do you mean? Marthe asked.

I mean like, are you someone's cousin or niece or something?

No, we're not related, Marthe said.

Oh, Kara said. Okay. Oh look, I think that's them. She set her coffee cup down and stood up; she trotted down the couple of steps and waved down the road. That's the boys there now, she said, turning back to Marthe.

A truck backed in, close to the steps, and two guys got out. Marthe recognized the young bearded one who had come asking Ruth to sing at the fundraiser, and the other guy had to be one of the actors, he was tall, with that kind of larger-than-life beauty that Marthe associated with film and television people. Marthe stood apart as the three of them laughed and chatted about the night before, about meeting up after the show that night, about how if Kara was still around next week, they could get someone to take her out in the boat if she wanted. Marthe bent and picked up their coffee cups off the steps. This is Marthe, Kara said finally, pointing, and Marthe took a few steps closer, nodding at the guys. Hey, she said.

You up from the States too? the bearded boy said.

No, I'm from here, Marthe said quickly. Well, I mean, not here here, but from Newfoundland. She took another step closer. But the guy just said oh right on. He said cool, so should we get moving on this? We're running around like crazy here today.

They loaded the chairs in the pan of the truck and Kara said I guess we'll just come behind you on foot. If you can unload them at the theatre, we'll set them up. She looked at Marthe for confirmation. Right?

Marthe nodded.

At the theatre, Marthe immediately started working from the back of the hall, setting up the chairs in slightly curved rows, moving a little more quickly than was necessary. Kara watched her for a beat and then dragged a stack to the front, near the stage area, and started in there. They worked in silence until they had both made their way to the centre of the hall. Kara stood back and looked at the room. I don't think we left enough space between the rows, actually, she said. She started pulling one of Marthe's rows farther ahead. Marthe gritted her teeth and fell into step behind her, yanking each chair in the next row a few inches forward, the metal scraping on the floor.

So, if you're not a cousin or a niece, then what's your deal? Kara said then, without turning to look back at Marthe.

What do you mean?

Jenny's been pretty tight-lipped, Kara said, looking up now. Which is unusual for her.

Marthe nodded, taking this in. Kara hadn't been let in. She straightened up a little.

I'm just here for the summer, Marthe said. Not sure after that.

Kara dragged a last chair into place in the front row and stood looking at the new arrangement. So, you're their helper or something? Or what. Interesting little operation they got going. Not sure how sustainable it is, but it's interesting. I'm tempted to stick around a little while longer, see how it all works, she said.

I'm not the helper, I'm learning, Marthe said quickly. I'm going to take over. This is bigger than you think it is.

This came out in a rush, Marthe was winding up now, overriding a vaguely familiar feeling of wondering whether she was saying too much. She told Kara about Trish's mother, and Trish, and the Chicago Jane and her own Jane, she was proud and defensive and relishing the moment of telling this girl what was what. Kara remained quiet and unmoved while Marthe was speaking.

Yeah, I mean I knew some of that, she said finally.

Right, Marthe said.

Do you think there's Wi-Fi here? I need to check something and I'm running out of data.

Marthe left the theatre and walked back to Therese's, and thought about it, and decided that given everything Jenny had said that time about how we were all complex beings and friction was inevitable and really the thing that mattered was that they were all on the same side pushing for the same thing, that given all of that it was okay to think that Kara was a stuck-up bitch.

53.

Marthe let Therese mother her a little for a few days. She told her to tell the others she was sick, when Ruth came around looking for her for work, when Jenny came wondering if she wanted to come for dinner with her and Kara, it was Kara's last night in town, they were going to have a night out to see her off. She just needed a break, Marthe told herself. There was a lot to digest, she told herself. At least Kara was finally going. Marthe sat next to Therese while she watched her shows at night and then stared at her phone when Therese went up to bed. She tried to consider the possibilities. The possibility of getting a place out in St. John's. The possibility of going back to Montreal. The possibility of staying on here indefinitely, finding something to occupy herself for the winter when the tourist activity dried up and the place went quiet for months on end. Maybe she could get a job at the restaurant. Maybe she could make an effort in town, socially.

Eventually she skulked back to Trish's late one night and just went up to bed. She was dressed and ready in the morning when Ruth came down, Ruth just nodding at her and rattling off the agenda for the day. The pink house, the Kelly place, the one up behind the legion. Marthe didn't ask again about Labrador. They fell back into a rhythm, tentatively and then more easily. In the garden one evening, Trish looked over at Marthe and said it's just what she's like, you know. Ruth, that is. She believes in it as much as you or I do, she just can't sit still.

Marthe looked up.

It's just what she's like, Trish said again.

I know, Marthe said, and Trish nodded and they went back to pulling carrots.

And then one morning about a week or so after Kara's departure, Ruth rapped on Marthe's bedroom door. It was early, a day off for them. She poked her head in the room when Marthe answered. We've got a problem, she said. Ms. Academia sold us out.

Marthe stared at her. For fuck sakes, she said. She got out of bed and reached for a sweater and followed Ruth downstairs.

Jenny was in the kitchen. Anxious, almost in tears. Kara had published an article. Not an academic paper, she'd written an article for a feminist magazine detailing her adventures in outsider reproductive health. She had gone to Spain and met the GynePunk women hacking reproductive technology, making speculums with 3D printers and testing their own fluids. She had interviewed the women in California who'd invented the cannula syringe. And she had gone to rural Newfoundland and had an at-home abortion by an old midwife who claimed to be working in the tradition of Jane.

But I didn't tell her any of that stuff, Jenny said. I swear. It was on a need-to-know basis, as always.

Marthe's swagger started replaying in her head.

I did, I talked to her, Marthe said.

What the fuck, Marthe, Ruth snapped.

I know, I'm sorry. I should have realized, but she was saying all this stuff, and I just.

Trish was calm. She hadn't gotten up from the kitchen table.

She didn't name the town, or any of us, she said. Nobody who reads that thing is even going to know where Newfoundland is.

But, the internet, Marthe said. It doesn't matter where it was published if that thing gets shared around. Like didn't you say that girl's husband, the one with the baby, wasn't her husband suspicious?

If, worst case, they come and arrest me, say, Trish said, sure it'll only fuel the fire. Remember those women in Ireland who turned themselves in? The nice grannies, the sympathetic news stories? It'll be that.

Ruth cut in. What, where is this coming from?

I watch the news, Trish said. Do I think she should have written that? No, that was for herself and she knows that, deep down, so she can live with that.

Jenny said I am sorry guys, really, for bringing her up here. If I had known.

Ruth's ugly laugh. Marthe tasting something curdled in the back of her throat.

I did, though, Jenny paused, still hesitant. I did get the package when I brought her back out to the city for her flight. The pills.

Good, Trish said. Otherwise, we will just mind our business for a minute, Trish said. I just have one visit to make here this morning.

She looked at Marthe. You'll come with me. One more Jane visit and then we'll sit tight for a while.

54.

Marthe followed Trish out to the truck and they drove over to a little blue house, parking the truck down the road a ways. Marthe was silent, tears stinging at her eyes. Trish spoke to the windshield.

How long you planning on carrying that cross around?

What?

We're moving on now. It was a mistake, and now you know that. It happens. These things will happen.

Marthe nodded.

Trish handed her a big empty soup pot. Take this, she said.

What is it?

The appearance of soup, Trish said. The one across the street is as nosy as they come. This is Glenda Moores's place and her uncle just died so we are bringing soup.

Glenda Moores came to the door and accepted the empty pot. They followed her into the kitchen and she sat at the table, her body soft and crumpled. Trish got her a cup of tea. She'd given Marthe the lowdown in the truck. The husband worked away. He was possibly not in the know. They would not be asking any further questions on that front.

It would be good if we could get it over with sooner than later, Glenda said.

Yes, Trish said.

The kids are over at Mom's, but just till tonight, Glenda said.

Trish said okay, here is what we're going to do. She said I think you've had enough of being poked at. She said I have the pill, do you know about that? They'll have it everywhere soon enough and it won't be from the likes of me, I mean who knows, we'll see. But I think it's our best bet for you right now.

Trish said we'll stay with you. She said it is not exactly pleasant, but it is maybe less invasive. Glenda nodded and got up to answer the ringing phone.

Trish to Marthe: For all I know, this will be everywhere eventually. You'll get it at the pharmacy. Or, just as likely, they'll load it down with red tape and it'll be for city people only, or you'll have to get permission from some father-figure pharmacist or something. I rarely have it, but sometimes Jenny can get it, so we use it in certain cases, why not, but we just don't ever forget how to use our own hands.

Marthe nodded. Trish made soup in the empty pot and

when the cramps began and Glenda Moores was in sitting on her toilet cursing and moaning, Trish sat sturdy on the edge of the tub and gave Marthe orders. A glass of water. A damp cloth. Glenda, why don't we put some fresh sheets on the bed for you, that always feels good. You'll take a cool shower after all this and then the bed will be fresh and cool too.

By the time they left that evening, Glenda was sheet-white, exhausted, and fucking pissed. I'll be glad the day I'm too old for this, she said. But she let them essentially put her to bed.

Marthe was thinking about the boat doctor, the film, and her own disappointment that it all seemed so anticlimactic. They hadn't shown the gory bits. She said to Trish how she hadn't quite realized the pill still involved all that. Yes, Trish said. She said it's the kind of thing where doctors start pulling out every euphemism in the book. Good work today, you helped set her at ease.

55.

This second emergence of Jane brought Marthe back. Okay, okay, okay. Okay, yes, she was still pissed at the idea of being left behind by Ruth, okay, yes, she hated the thought of herself as just following along. She burned with shame at having clearly played right into Kara's hands. But things were happening. She felt useful. She would be armed and ready, and ready to arm others. Ruth said how they would just keep moving forward. Ruth said how they would figure it out.

Marthe had said but what about Labrador and Ruth had given her a look like I can't believe you're even asking me that.

Trish said now we need to sit still for a spell. See what comes of this. Marthe said but in the meantime. She said it feels like we just got momentum. Are they really going to come for you, I don't know, I can't think they'd really come for you.

Trish said there is something. We've got more pills coming. A real supply this time, Jenny worked it out.

Jane would go on the road. They would blend with the tourists out to visit the pretty little polished-up outports and they would keep a low profile in the shitty towns nobody visited. They would keep to the isolated bits. They would find a Jane in each area. She would be the keeper of the pills, she would hold a space for anyone who needed it. They would set her up, they would walk her through it. A network of Janes to own this version of the procedure so that anyone in town could own it too. Here's how to fly under the radar, here's what to expect, here's a number to call if you need it. Here is our approach: we undertake this together. We share the ownership, we share the responsibility. Jane would return another time with more skills to share. The pills a stopgap in the meantime. This was control. This was not resting easy in any trust of laws made primarily by men in the interest of their careers or in any trust that the weather and the climate weren't about to turn on them for real, stranding small communities that had lost the skills to survive in isolation. Did their new Janes know it was all actually quite simple? Did they know there was a reason it was so hard to find that out? Even when you held a world of information in a palm-sized device. It had been successfully cloaked so that they could never own it. Jane was here to whisk a curtain away.

Marthe said to Ruth you'll stay now, won't you? Marthe said to Ruth let's not go back.

When Trish gets arrested the narrative is all wrong, of course. It is not the point Trish was ever trying to make, though it is at least related. Trish will be made to seem a last resort, a frightening prospect. See, they will say. Look at what rural women are forced to do. Look at the risk they will take. This is why we need more doctors and more clinics; this is why we need that pill readily available. They will shroud all details to the contrary, they will neglect to find and talk to anyone who actually experienced the procedure at Trish's strong hands. They will make it frightful. They will wonder if it was for money, they will hint at her mother's dark past. The town will hesitate in its relentless self-promotion and the mayor will amp up the bright positivity, he will say things in the media about welcoming young doctors back home, he will never say Trish's name, nobody will, they will plug the vitality, the young families, the new restaurants. There will be shots of tow-headed children in pink rubber boots picking up capelin on the news and Ruth and Marthe will shut the television off and make plans. Therese will be the go-between for the minute they keep Trish in custody, and then Trish will be let go for lack of any real evidence, for lack of anyone willing to testify, for lack of commitment on the part of the Crown attorneys who decide in the end that it isn't terribly worth the shitstorm to try and prosecute her.

Jenny will make a feature film. She will go home to New York and abandon her documentaries and write and direct a feature film that posits a tiny utopia amid the undeniable dystopic mess her country has fallen into. She will set this utopia on a small island off the coast, where a midwife seeks an apprentice to keep up the work, to offer the procedure made all but illegal again just as people start to really fear bringing children into a world grown hotter and stormier and ever more precarious for human life. The island will lose contact with the mainland country due to sudden tropical storms.

And Ruth and Marthe will drive on. They will go home to Trish, keep the light on over the back door.

I'll stay, yes, Ruth said to Marthe. But here is the thing. Here is what we do. We set it up, we create the network, we leave a number to call and we always always answer, but we otherwise disappear. If we hang on to anything it's that Jane has no one face. Jane a great, shifting, multitudinous thing.

56.

The damage control in the town paid off and it became known as a thriving example of what happened when people came home, decided to live smaller, slower lives. The mayor was a vocal proponent of the new provincial midwifery legislation and a nice hippie-ish woman from Ontario was installed in town and the young townies just moved back out to the bay lined up at her door. The province was rich again and everyone forgot how quickly things would inevitably swing back around again. They bought houses and land, they started expensive new ventures. A bunch of aging punks from the city moved into a place down the road from Trish and started gathering and processing seaweed. The government would throw millions into doomed projects, the province would collapse and then struggle to its feet again, the town's fortunes would rise and fall and rise and fall. The Ontario midwife would get sick of the weather and the isolation and leave, and people would slowly trickle back to Trish, on the quiet. The island would elect conservative old businessmen and then it would elect some fresh young voice. The country would swing back and forth in a staggered echo of the monolith beneath it. And eventually, regardless of any of this, the weather would assert its power, it would turn on them. The tourists would retreat. And Trish would be ready.

Marthe and Ruth knew this to be the future. Marthe still felt bent on control, but that urge had now found its locus. She remembered her posture in love, cupping the flame of a thing. They, Jane, would amass a network that would huddle to cup and protect this one measure of control.

This was the story Marthe told herself. She was writing the story of Jane as they were still living it out, but that was the only way she knew how to be in the world. The future perfect, how it will have been, a fierce story, a story of endurance. Marthe wanted it to have been real. Marthe wanted to have put her hands to work in the world and Jane was the way to do that. This she had decided long before, but there is always the moment when the decision is made real. Marthe was wrist-deep in the earnest mission now. Marthe was allowing herself the grandiose.

Jane would insist it never be euphemistic. Jane would cut no corners on truth. Jane was here to hold one hand as the other touched a dark and necessary place.

57.

In the days after the article is released, Marthe walked back up the hill for more blueberries, squatting here and there until her legs ached and her bucket was dusty full. Walking home, she heard a racket around the corner. The mummer's parade. Marthe had scoffed at the idea. Mummering was for the winter night, it was a dark revelry, an inversion ritual. Mummering had been made illegal in town years ago because the rich were afraid of the rowdy, masked drunk. They'd revived it out here for a Christmas afternoon, and then they realized they were missing an opportunity, the tourists, so they'd cleaned it up for the bright summer daytime. The mummers turned into clowns, the dark but joyous ritual made into a kind of Halloween Mardi Gras for tourists. But now they rounded the bend and surrounded her, laughing and shouting, someone wailing on an out-of-tune ukulele, yes, in the full light of an August afternoon, yes, but Marthe felt a panic rising despite herself, it was disconcerting still, the garish covered faces, the distorted shrieks. She stopped and let them flood around her, fixing a smile.

58.

At Trish's, they held council. They laid out one plan in the event of this, and another in the event of that. They were five. The others took their cue from Trish and they were calm. There were options. These were all what-ifs. This was always a possibility. We have dealt with this before, to one extent or another. The thing to remember was that a lot of people had a stake in this. The thing to remember was that a lot of it was politics and optics on the part of the people who held the power. The thing to remember was that they were out in the middle of the Atlantic on an island on an earth simmering with heat and rage and people would have to see that they were eventually, once again, going to have to fend for themselves.

Marthe felt she had never seen so clearly. Jane was a story of fending for themselves. Jane was a story of doing it anyway. Jane was a story of getting away with it. Of implication. Of we're all in this together. Jane was a story of inescapable bodies. Jane was a locus of control in a world that was hurtling. Jane was a story of passing not one torch but many. Jane a great, shifting, multitudinous thing.

Trish made a pot of stew and they all ate heaping plates, suddenly ravenous. Trish set a bottle of whiskey on the table. This was what they would do for the moment. That night the wind came up and it ripped off the roof of the theatre, it blew an old mattress up into a tree in the part of town the mayor liked to steer the cameras away from. It rained and rained and the water rose and the wind knifed sharp and the road into town washed out. They were left to themselves a moment longer, and they were ready.

Notes

"A pregnant woman is a woman who cannot escape herself" is from Guadalupe Muro's novel *Air Carnation*.

Angie Jackson chronicled her experience taking RU-486, the abortion pill, live on Twitter in 2010. Emily Letts filmed herself having a surgical abortion in 2014.

Tracey Emin spoke about her abortion in an interview with Hermann Vaske in 1999.

Aliza Shvarts described her project *Untitled [Senior Thesis]* as a piece that "exists only in its telling" in a 2008 *Yale Daily News* article. In an interview with *impactmania*, Shvarts said of the aftermath of her project, "It was a difficult moment, because every single MFA program rejected me. I had some extra phone interviews with one program, in which one of the deans got on the line and asked if I was 'sorry for what I did to Yale.'"

Acknowledgements

Much of what I learned about the Chicago Jane collective came from Laura Kaplan's invaluable and comprehensive history *The Story of Jane: The Legendary Underground Feminist Abortion Service*.

Other books that were helpful for understanding the history of abortion access and the fight for reproductive justice in Canada and the U.S. include *The Abortion Caravan* by Karin Wells; *Without Apology: Writings on Abortion in Canada*, edited by Sharon Stettner; *Abortion: History, Politics and Reproductive Justice after Morgentaler*, edited by Shannon Stettner, Kristin Burnett and Travis Hey; *Seizing the Means of Reproduction* by Michelle Murphy; and Catherine Dunphy's excellent and clear-eyed biography of Henry Morgentaler, *Morgentaler: A Difficult Hero*. On midwifery in Newfoundland, I turned to Janet McNaughton's doctoral dissertation "The Role of the Newfoundland Midwife in Traditional Healthcare, 1900 to 1970."

An early excerpt of *We, Jane* appeared in the journal *MuseMedusa* and I am very grateful to Geneviève Robichaud for the invitation to contribute and for her thoughtful and generative feedback on the text.

For conversation, inspiration and support in many forms: love and thanks to Amanda Power, Vanessa McGivern, Aleshia Jensen, Jodee Richardson, Luke Major, Caroline Marinacci, Jessica Hébert, Jon Montes, and Benjamin Langlois.

Thank you to my family for all of the above and more.

Malcolm Sutton is a sensitive and perceptive reader and the most thoughtful editor. I am very grateful for the attention and care he put into editing this novel, as well as for his beautiful cover design. It is a joy to work with Jay MillAr and Hazel Millar and I thank them for their enthusiasm and dedication. Much gratitude.

AIMEE WALL is a writer and translator. She has translated the novels *Testament* and *Drama Queens* by Vickie Gendreau and *Sports and Pastimes* by Jean-Philippe Baril Guérard, as well as *Prague* by Maude Veilleux, in a co-translation with Aleshia Jensen. Her translation of Alexie Morin's *Open Your Heart* is forthcoming in 2021. She is originally from Grand Falls-Windsor, Newfoundland, and currently lives in Montréal. *We, Jane* is her first novel.

Colophon

Manufactured as the first edition of *We, Jane.*
in the spring of 2021 by Book*hug Press

Edited for the press by Malcolm Sutton
Copy edited by Shannon Whibbs
Type + design by Malcolm Sutton

bookhugpress.ca

Book*hug Press